*"I love you, Karon," Jon whispered. "How I love you!"*

At one time his words would have made Karon the happiest woman alive. Now they added to her pain. They brought her worries spiraling back to the moment.

*". . . Jon!"*

Being so intimately in Jon's arms, while knowing in her heart it had to be the last time, made it a torment. Logically Karon knew she had to break it off, even as Jon embraced her soft body against his tall, angular frame.

*"Marry me, Karon. I want you for my wife, darling. Always. . . and forever."*

❧❧❧

**SUSAN FELDHAKE** lives with her family on a farm in Illinois. She writes many inspirational romances, and publishes ROMANTIC TIDINGS for Inspirational Readers & Writers, from her Watson home, when time and family obligations permit.

*Polly Bishop*

# *Reflection Of Love*

## *Susan C. Feldhake*

*Christmas 1986
from Melvia*

**HARVEST HOUSE PUBLISHERS**
Eugene, Oregon 97402

**Other Rhapsody Romance Books:**

# REFLECTION OF LOVE

Copyright © 1984 by Susan Feldhake
Published by Harvest House Publishers
Eugene, Oregon 97402

ISBN 0-89081-420-1

**Printed in the United States of America.**

For my darling little "Sylvie Bear,"
born January 12, 1983,
who cooed and kept me happy company,
a beautiful reflection of love. . .
while I wrote **Reflection of Love.**

# Chapter One

*T*wenty-four-year-old Karon Kirlin brushed a wisp of curly blonde hair away from her tanned face and cocked her head as she poised before her father's workbench, listening.

It *was* the doorbell!

Wiping her hands on the seat of her jeans Karon scurried from the basement as the doorbell shrilled insistently.

Karon crossed to the front door of the home which had belonged to her parents until their death, and now was hers. It was Saturday afternoon, and Karon opened the front door expecting to confront a round-faced child selling cookies, magazine subscriptions, garden seeds, or other club fund-raising project item.

Instead, her boyfriend, twenty-seven-year-old Jonathan Wingate, lounged against the door frame, waiting. He hadn't been due in from his business trip until Monday.

"Jon!" Karon gasped, surprised.

"None other," Jon admitted, smiling. "And you're Miss Muffet, I presume?" he teased and pulled a sticky gray spider web from Karon's tangled hair.

Karon looked at the silken web and shuddered as Jon worked it free from his fingertips and dropped it to the grass.

"The basement was an absolute mess. But it's empty now. All that remains is . . . the rest of the house." Karon gave a soft groan when she comprehended what work still faced her. Karon dropped to the plush windowseat to get a moment's rest. "I don't know how I'll ever get done on time, Jon. I wish the people who contracted to buy the house hadn't been so eager to take possession." She faced him. "I never dreamed it would rush me so to meet the date we agreed on."

"I know," Jon said in an understanding voice. "That's why I came dressed to help."

Karon rolled her blue eyes as Jon sat on the ledge beside her and wrapped her in his arms, pulling her head to his shoulder. She snuggled close.

"I've had your help before!"

Jon laughed. "Okay. But this time I'll keep my mind on packing—not on you."

Karon uncrossed her slim legs, left Jon's embrace, and stiffly arose to face further packing.

"Well, see that you do!" she warned in a chipper voice. "I've got quite enough distractions as it is."

Jon frowned. "I don't know if that's a compliment or an insult."

Karon grinned. "Consider it a compliment."

"All right, if you say so, I will. It's nice to know you find me distracting." The handsome architect looked suddenly mystified. "But, distractingly... *what?*"

"Hmmmm... let me see," Karon said, wrinkling her brow in thought. "Distractingly handsome, charming, nice, appealing, witty, lovable." Jon laughed, pleased.

"You are *disarmingly* complimentary, you flatterer!"

Worry settled over Karon's features. "And this house is *disgustingly* messy."

"We'll have it whipped in no time," Jon promised. "When the contractor couldn't make our weekend meeting, I took the next flight back to Chicago so I could help you. What do you want me to do?" Jon gave a mock bow and kissed Karon's grubby hand. "At your service, madame..."

"You don't mind?" Karon asked.

"Of course not, or I wouldn't be here."

"You could box up the books," Karon suggested. "I promised them to a veterans' hospital."

"Will do," Jon agreed, crossing to the shelves. "Are there any you care to save?"

"No. My books are at the apartment. Discard them all."

Jon set to work and the two faced their tasks, chatting comfortably. Karon sorted out the personal items collected over forty years of her parents' marriage, filling large boxes with things to be hauled away by the charities. A small pile contained the items Karon chose to keep.

"You'll want to keep this book, won't you?"

"No," Karon answered without bothering to look. "I truly don't have room for any more books. Whatever it is—give it away!"

"You're sure?" Jon questioned in an astounded tone. Karon looked and saw Jon admiring an ornate box. She sighed. It was going to take longer if she had to stop and pass judgment on every book Jon touched.

"What is it?" Karon asked in a flat voice.

"A Bible." Jon opened the box. "Your family Bible."

"Oh."

"You'll want to keep it, won't you?" Jon asked.

"Okay, keep it if you want to," Karon said. She held up yellowing lace doilies, realized her mother hadn't crocheted them, and put the handiwork in a box to be given away. Karon felt Jon's eyes on her, puzzled and assessing.

"It doesn't matter what *I* want . . . it's what *you* want! You don't have to keep the Bible if you don't want to, Karon. I'm sure it would find appreciative readers at the veterans' hospital."

Karon suffered a twinge of embarrassment. She hadn't realized how she must have sounded.

"Put it with my things," Karon decided quietly, putting an end to the discussion.

Karon turned back to her work but once more she was bothered by the thorny issue that regularly sprang up between her and Jon, pricking her contentment.

Karon had never known such happiness as she had experienced when Jon came into her life shortly before her aged mother died, following the death of her father, four years earlier.

Although she and Jon had been dating more than six months, sometimes Karon was bothered by the fact that in such surprisingly short time Jon had so completely filled her life that she worried he had come to mean more to her than he really should. And more times than Karon cared to admit, she grew concerned that she did not mean as much to Jon as she had hoped she would.

Karon found herself drawn to Jon, not just because of his tanned good looks, generous, quick grin, kind manner, or pleasant sense of humor. But somehow he appealed to her in ways she had never been attracted to a man before.

Karon glanced at Jon, who was sitting cross-legged on the floor, thumbing through the Bible, the task at hand momentarily forgotten. Karon felt stung when she was forced to admit Jonathan Wingate's Christianity was more precious to him than she was!

Karon had been aware of Jon's faith and commitment almost from the moment they first met. In many ways she saw it as a blessing. Jon didn't smoke, so he wasn't burning holes in her clothing or furniture. Jonathan didn't drink liquor and get loud, act silly, or become brazen and surly. Jon didn't tell her dirty jokes and expect her to appreciate them and entertain him in kind. Jon expected no more from their date than her company and conversation.

That side of Jon's religion, Karon appreciated. The other?

Karon felt ashamed that she seemed helpless to prevent the sense of embarrassment she suffered when Jon bowed his head in restaurants and offered silent thanks before he ate. Karon wondered if everyone in the room was staring at them and whispering. Other times, when Jon spoke in public and private about "the Lord," as if this God of his was as individual as one of their friends, Karon grew uncomfortable.

As much as she had come to love Jon, Karon hated to realize that others might be laughing at him behind his back. Jon was so good, so kind, and so decent that Karon felt petty and disloyal when she experienced the flickerings of embarrassment caused by Jon's expressions of faith.

It wasn't that Karon considered herself against religion. She wasn't. It was just that she thought it unusual when people were so *public* about it. Almost everyone Karon knew had some kind of religious affiliation and believed in some kind of "god."

Karon felt she had her own beliefs, too, although she admitted she didn't know them well enough to state them when Jon once questioned her about her ideals.

"I haven't given it much thought," Karon dismissed Jon's questions, relieved when he changed the subject. Karon had feared he would seize the opportunity to press his beliefs on her because he was so firm in his faith. There were so many religions—cults, too—composed of sincere, devoted people, as firm in the conviction theirs was the right faith, as Jon was staunch in his ideas. Karon found it all rather confusing.

When Jon glanced up from the Kirlin family Bible and saw the forlorn look on Karon's face, he misread it, and decided the frown was caused by his musings when he had promised to help.

"Sorry, sweetheart!" Jon apologized with a grin. He placed the Bible on the pile of family mementos. "What next?"

"Probably a side trip to an insane asylum," Karon joked, sighing. "When I realize how much I have left to do—I think I'll go crazy."

"It's not that bad," Jon comforted.

"No, not merely bad. . . worse! Jon, I don't see how I can possibly be done in time to go to your parents' cabin next weekend."

Jon said nothing for a long moment. "Today is only Saturday. You'll make it."

"I'm not so sure," Karon said, hesitating. "I hate to ask, Jon. . . but do you think we could make the trip another time?"

"No!" Jon was firm. He offered several reasons why they couldn't change their plans to travel to the Wingate vacation home for Karon's first visit.

"Forget I even mentioned it!" Karon said crisply, and set a filled box down a little harder than necessary. Jon halted his work to eye her, then went to her and hugged Karon with understanding. Although Karon didn't resist his touch, she remained wooden.

Jon kissed her temple. "I know you're worried, hon. If you really think you won't make the deadline, I'll arrange to help every night after work this week."

Jon's patience made Karon's unusual moodiness seem all the more unreasonable.

"Please forget I suggested a change in plans," Karon said again weakly.

When they set to work once more, Karon found she couldn't put the upcoming trip from her mind. She knew that she would be done with the boxing and packaging. Using the disposal of her parents' estate was only an excuse that might have postponed an occasion that caused her both eagerness and apprehension. By taking her to meet his family, Karon sensed Jon was signaling an intention that one day he might choose her to be his wife.

Such a relationship with Jon was one she both desired and feared. Some days she wished with all her heart to marry Jon, to be all the things she wanted to become to a man she loved. Other times she feared the very thought of a permanent commitment to a man who loved his Lord more than he seemed to care for her.

Jon and Karon worked steadily all afternoon. Jon pointed out the strong possibility that Karon would finish the job with time to spare.

"I've got to go," Jon said when evening came, after Karon shared her packed lunch with him.

"I won't work much longer myself," she responded.

Jon paused. "You don't mind if I leave now? I have some calls to make."

"Go ahead," Karon assured, accepting his parting kiss. "And thanks, Jon. Thanks for somehow always being there when I need you."

"Sure thing," Jon whispered. "Any time. . . ."

Karon didn't work long after Jonathan drove away in his black Porsche. She went to the basement to assure herself that it, at least, was empty and ready for the new owners to occupy.

Karon started up the stairs. Turning to yank the dangling cord that hung from the glaring light bulb, a flash of metal winked at her from the space between the dusty floor joists. Karon shielded her eyes and squinted. The glint wasn't light reflecting on a nail. Something was tucked into the space created where boards butted against each other!

Karon stood on her tiptoes, fumbling to explore the crevice, when she touched a metal box and plucked it from its resting place.

Like a child at Christmas, Karon held the box to her ear and shook it. She was rewarded by a muffled thud and the swishy sound of rustling papers.

*Money!?*

Karon's heart skipped a beat before logic abolished the thought. Her parents had no treasure trove hidden in the basement. The Kirlins hadn't been poor, but neither had they been wealthy. Had there been a store of cash or valuables, her mother certainly would have told her about it when pressing bills due to her mother's illness made it necessary to remortgage the house.

Clutching the box to her, Karon gave the joists a cursory glance, then skittered up the stairs and slammed the door behind her.

Upstairs the box refused to open. Karon was forced to set it aside until she could take it home and find the right tools and a can of lubricating oil. Karon locked the bungalow to return to her apartment which she shared with a friend, Midge Harper, in a singles complex.

All the way home the metal box seemed to exude a foreboding air. Karon wondered if it was foolish for the unopened box to cause such conflicting fears within her: fear that she would be disappointed in the inconsequential contents, or worse, fear that she would find something of such value it would disrupt her very life.

The soft-spoken, hard-working, upstanding man her father had been, there was no chance the box would be full of smutty pictures. And the idea of finding brittle, yellowing newspaper clippings that revealed her mother as a paroled criminal was laughable.

Even so, the chill remained.

At her apartment, Karon set the box on the kitchen table, oiled the hinges, grabbed a screwdriver and hammer, and with several solid whacks, jarred the hasps free. The lid creaked when she tried to force it open.

At that instant Karon fought down an almost paralyzing desire to throw the box down the incinerator chute. She held the box in her trembling hands and glanced toward the door where the chute awaited, just a few doors down.

Shouldn't she, Karon thought, after having already discarded box after box of trivia collected by her parents? What harm could come in casting the box away with the contents unexamined? Karon grew cautious. There was the chance the box held valuables—stocks, bonds, certificates.

The dank, musty smell of aged papers filled the air when Karon forced the lid back. She looked into the box and didn't know if she felt relief or disappointment as she shoved aside cancelled checks, an old bank book, documents, some letters. . . .

Just as she thought, Karon decided as she examined an outdated refrigerator warranty card and a deer hunting license. Old forgotten junk! She dug deeper.

Karon's lips parted in horror. Slowly, piece by piece she fit the odd collection of papers together, hurriedly skimming the contents, comparing the dates and events that meshed together in her mind.

Her parents had carefully created a life for her! They had purposely kept from her their secret past! Karon's blue eyes tingled with tears. Her parents had claimed they lived in Chicago—always and forever—but they hadn't! They had lied to her. But why? *Why?*

Knowing she had no choice, Karon examined each item in detail. Like jigsaw puzzle pieces, when arranged in the right order, the items gave a picture of what had taken place almost a quarter of a century before.

A hot tear scalded down Karon's cheek to be followed by another, and another, before she closed the box and knew that the story created in the strongbox was true. It was the life she had lived with her parents that was the lie.

Story after story her parents had related to her about her birth, of Karon being the miracle baby born to them late in life. Lies! Untruths told, perhaps out of love and a desire to protect Karon and themselves, but lies, regardless, and the outcome was cruel deception.

Karon knew now she hadn't been the miracle baby her mother claimed her to be, grown beneath Dorothy Kirlin's middle-aged heart. The papers in the strongbox proved that! Karon had been conceived by a nameless woman; nurtured under the cold, hard heart of a woman who had not wanted her; a woman who bore her, but found a solution in selling the newborn babe to a desperate, aging couple who purchased the girl child as the answer to their dreams.

The move to Chicago, no doubt, had been a calculated attempt to find anonymity in the sprawling, impersonal city. A plan to thwart anyone who might try at a later date to find the Kirlins and legally reclaim the child.

Karon was thankful Midge was out when she began to sob without control. An hour later, drained, Karon made her way to the telephone. She flipped over the charity's business card to find the worker's home telephone number jotted on back.

In a calm voice that contrasted with her ravaged face, Karon instructed the worker that the key to the Kirlin home could be obtained from the realty office, and the home was to be emptied of all the remaining contents as soon as possible.

"Everything?" the worker asked.

"Everything but the books. Someone from the veteran's hospital will claim them."

When she hung up Karon hoped she wouldn't regret the decision. But now, knowing what she did, going through her parents' personal effects would be a pain too great to bear. Anyway, she had all the things she knew she wanted to keep and eventually would cherish. Along with those things was a box of secrets that were hers to regret.

It was late when Midge returned to the apartment after a date. Karon was up and composed, although her eyes were red from crying.

Midge, a brusk newspaper reporter, a year older than Karon, with a cheerful face, short russet hair, and frank eyes, missed nothing. Midge, noted for her abrupt demeanor, passed up a chance to comment and Karon was grateful that for once Midge chose to say nothing.

Karon needed time to think. Time to get over the shock. Time in which to start feeling like a person rather than a nonentity. Karon feared she wouldn't have the time she wanted... *needed.* After all, they were only days away from the planned visit to the Wingates.

Before, Karon had felt merely nervous about the visit. Now, she suffered agony at the thought. How could she face it? How could she hope to make a decent impression on the Wingates as devastated as she felt?

"God only knows," Karon murmured miserably, as she slipped between the cool sheets. She tried not to think about the situation and she tried harder to sleep, but succeeded at neither. Softly Karon turned aside to bury her face in her pillow so Midge wouldn't hear as she cried until exhaustion finally stilled her in restless sleep.

# Chapter Two

*T*he remainder of the week passed too quickly to suit Karon. Jon was busy so she sensed his relief when she announced his help wasn't needed because she had already disposed of the contents of her parents' estate.

Friday arrived and with it came the weekend Karon had come to dread. The few times Jon had telephoned during the week, he was so eager to visit his parents and see his sister, Liz that Karon hoped his attitude would be infectious, making the visit a weekend to enjoy rather than one to endure.

Midge didn't miss the apprehension etched into Karon's features when her roommate waited for Jon to arrive.

"You're going to have a wonderful weekend. Lucky you to escape the city heat for lakeside cool," Midge said. "You'll hate to come home."

"I hope so." Karon's smile was too quick. Her words too glum. Midge Harper frowned.

"Being nervous and moody isn't like you, Karon," Midge observed. "You've been like this for..." she hesitated. "Well, for almost a week now. What gives?"

Karon feigned surprise, shrugged, and gave Midge a silent, nervous grin. When Karon presented no answer, Midge pursed her mouth and lifted an eyebrow.

"What happened to the poised, confident girl I thought I shared an apartment with? Who's this glum, miserable stranger I keep tripping over in the kitchen and living room?"

Midge's manner was almost too much to bear. Karon was tempted to pour it all out. But her desire to keep her secret hidden, as it had been for twenty-four years, was the stronger instinct. Karon swallowed hard.

"I-I don't know what you're talking about," she stammered weakly.

"Baloney!" Midge snorted. The reporter's attitude hinted that she wasn't about to give up until she had a better answer.

"I suppose I'm tense about meeting Jon's family," Karon presented an explanation. "Jon means so much to me, I suppose it's natural to want his folks to like me and to be a bit worried that maybe they won't for some reason."

Midge sniffed. "What reason, pray tell?" She dismissed Karon's fear as ridiculous. "They're Jon's parents—not some kind of royalty. You don't have a worry in the world," Midge predicted. "From my own limited experience, which is vastly more than yours, I can tell you exactly what the weekend will be like. Mosquitoes the size of helicopters will hover in the air. Antique plumbing in the drafty cottage will go on the blink and stay that way for the duration. Although the local weatherman predicts warm and sunny weather for the tri-state area, don't believe it! It will probably rain the whole time and the roof will leak. Between thundershowers you can eat hamburgers—because the fish won't bite. The burgers, of course, will be marinated in beach sand, and grilled—no, make that *charred*—by none other than Buck Wingate who will regale—make that *bore*—you with stories about his high school years when he was on the football team. He'll still wear his letterman's sweater to prove it." Midge rolled her eyes expressively. "And Jon's mother—what's her name?"

"Pepper," Karon furnished.

Midge nodded and didn't miss a beat. "Right, while Pepper, who didn't come by the name dishonestly, will slosh jalepeno pepper sauce on the hamburgers and anything else that gets in her way.''

Karon laughed in spite of herself and the gloomy feelings she couldn't seem to shake. Midge grinned with satisfaction.

''That situation strikes fear in your lovestruck heart, dear friend? Fie! Where's your sense of adventure? You've nothing to fear from the Wingates, Karon, unless it's that they'll all be so wild about you they won't let Jon return you from the Wisconsin Wilderness to Civilized Chicago. Now that, pal, is something to be concerned about.''

The doorbell interrupted Midge's chatter. Karon crossed the room to let Jon in. He brushed a kiss across her forehead, smiled at Midge, and reached for Karon's luggage.

''Ready to go?'' Jon asked.

''As ready as she'll ever be,'' Midge answered for Karon and tucked her pencil behind her ear as she adjusted her reading glasses.

Startled, Jon gave Midge a measured look, but said nothing, mainly because, as usual, talkative Midge gave him no chance. She wrinkled her nose and gave Karon a fond, exasperated look.

''Karon's been acting like a lamb being led off to slaughter. I keep telling her that Wingates don't eat pretty travel agents. Uh. . .do they?'' Midge questioned cautiously.

"No," Jon said, laughing.

"Midge!" Karon said sharply. She tried to catch her roommate's eye to give her a pointed look.

"Once Karon gets to the lake she'll find out I'm right," Midge rattled on, either missing Karon's warning glance or choosing to ignore it. "As I've always said, and someone more famous than I said before me: 'There's nothing to fear but fear itself.' "

"Right, Midge," Jon said patiently. "If we don't hurry, I *fear* we'll get hopelessly tangled in traffic and never get to my parents' home." Jon led the way to his car. "That Midge," he said amused. "What a nut!"

Karon felt anything but amused. She fumed in silent embarrassment as Jon stowed her luggage in his car.

The Porsche was the only area where Karon knew Jon to splurge, other than dressing well because of his job. Karon assumed Jon paid for his car with installments like most people did. His apartment, where Jon lived alone, was even similiar to the one where Karon and Midge resided.

"Is Midge getting you down?" Jon asked lightly when Karon's heavy sigh broke the stillness in the car.

"Oh, not really. . ." Karon's drab voice was unconvincing.

Jon squeezed her hand and gave her an encouraging smile. "You know how Midge is. She means well. She loves you like a sister. Sure, she can be brash and outspoken. God knows I'm aware of that!" Jon laughed at the memory. "But Midge Harper's heart is in the right place."

"Don't remind me!" Karon said, groaning.

But her mind was already pulled back to the first time Midge met Jon.

Good old Midge had been at her brassiest best that night. Karon tried—but failed—to keep her date with Jon a secret. She hoped that Midge would be out of the apartment when Jon came to pick her up. She didn't want to chance Midge's opinionated statements or rash comments costing her a new friend.

The best laid plans can go awry. Midge, through no fault of her own, found her plans cancelled, so she was firmly entrenched in the apartment doing her fingernails when Jon arrived. Karon had no choice but to make introductions.

"Wingate?" Midge cried. She sat up and her eyes narrowed with a look that Karon correctly surmised meant a barrage of questions were about to follow.

"Wingate?" the reporter repeated. She assessed Jon with frank interest. And as usual, Midge Harper, reporter, got right to the heart of the matter. "Who are your parents?"

Jon gave Midge an easy smile while Karon stared miserably at her shoes, her mind reeling with sharp words she would like to say to get Midge to quit interrogating Jon. Why, Midge was acting as if she *might* let Karon leave the apartment with him if he answered the questions to her satisfaction.

"My parents? Buck and Pepper Wingate," Jon said. "Do you . . . know them?"

Midge's expression was one of disappointment. "Nope," she sighed. " 'Fraid not. I thought for a minute you might be one of the important Wingates. You know . . . *the* Wingates. The millionaire, manufacturing Wingates. They're all over the society page. I should've known better, though," Midge rambled on. "You're probably too pleasant and too common for them. Kitty, the editor of the society page, says that Mrs. Wingate is pure snob. I don't know if it's true or not," Midge admitted. "But it wouldn't surprise me. Kitty's used to dealing with VIPs and she calls 'em as she sees 'em."

Jon looked like he was struggling to form some kind of polite response. Before either he or Karon could frame a hasty reply and exit, Midge rattled on.

"I should have known you weren't one of *the* Wingates, what with your career," she explained further. "You'd be a vice president in Wingate

Manufacturing if you were, not a young and struggling architect working your way up from the bottom of the heap." Midge sighed with teasing sympathy. "Poor you. A working stiff like the rest of us. It looks that all you have in common with *those* Wingates is a name."

For Jon's sake, Karon's cheeks burned. She didn't dare glance at him, although she knew he was too much of a gentleman to bristle at Midge's remarks.

"Now that Midge has assured you that you're not about to go to dinner with one of *those* Wingates, may I still count on your keeping my poor, humble company?" Jon asked winking broadly.

Relief flooded over Karon. "Of course! What's in a name?"

"When you're a Wingate," Midged piped up, *"millions."*

Karon was scarcely aware of the world around her as Jon downshifted and jockeyed for a better position in the crush of Friday afternoon traffic leaving the city. Karon thought about Midge's weekend predictions, then tried to figure out for herself what would await her from the past information Jon has shared about his family. Startled, Karon realized that while she had talked on at length about herself, always at Jon's urging, he had been rather silent about his own family. In fact, Karon knew almost nothing about his family except for what Midge had wedged out of him.

"What does your father do, Jon? And your mother? Do they both work?" Karon finally spoke.

Jonathan gave Karon a perturbed look "What?" he asked quietly.

"I'd like to know about your parents. It just struck me that you've never spoken very much about them. Tell me what your dad and mother are like, so I'll know what to expect."

"What's left to tell that you don't already know?" Jon murmured.

Karon's lips parted. "Why...almost everything!" she pointed out. "It just dawned on me that I know nothing about your parents except what Midge browbeat out of you." Karon paused for breath. "I'd like to know a bit about them."

Jon's hazel eyes were perplexed. His gaze contained a mixture of puzzlement and indecision, then expectancy, as if he waited for Karon to deliver the punch line to a joke. When she did not, Jon uttered a sickly groan that chilled Karon to the marrow.

"Are you trying to tell me you don't know who I am? Who my parents are? Come on, Karon!"

Karon felt hurt by the unbelieving tone of his voice. "Of course I know who you are! Jonathan Wingate, architect, age twenty-seven. Parents—Buck and Pepper; sister—Liz; born in—"

"You really *don't* know," Jon broke in incredulously.

"Know *what*?" Karon asked, feeling as if she had walked into an engrossing movie late, unprepared for the dramatic action, and no one would clue her in.

Jon groaned again. He rubbed his palm on his forehead and shook his head in disbelief.

"Karon, I thought all along you knew *exactly* who I am, or I wouldn't have been making such a joke out of it all this time. I *am,* to quote a friend of ours, one of *the* Wingates. I thought you knew that, and we were playing our own private little trick on Midge talking about . . . *the* Wingates in the joking way we did."

Karon's voice cracked. Her heart stopped beating. A numb feeling tingled through her. "You are one of *the Wingates*?"

Jon forced a weak smile. "You needn't make it sound like a shameful social disease."

Karon stared in horror. "Jon, no! Tell me you're not serious. Tell me you're not . . . who . . . you . . . are."

Karon's words faltered, then faded away. Tears sprang to her eyes. Jon flushed and shifted uncomfortably. Awkwardly he patted her hand as she fumbled for a tissue.

"Karon, honey . . . sweetheart . . . I'm sorry. Truly I am. If I had any idea you didn't know, I would have told you long ago. But I couldn't see any point in talking about my family when I figured you probably read the boring details in the newspaper's society page. I was more interested in learning about you.''

Karon's thoughts reeled. ''Then your parents are Warren and...''

''Althea,'' Jon said. He saw the look of despair settle over Karon's features. ''I didn't make up the other names to throw Midge off,'' he defended. ''To close friends, Mom and Dad are Buck and Pepper. I used their nicknames because if Midge knew the family well, she would recognize them. I usually do that. It eliminates a lot of problems and explanations. See?''

Karon nodded. She did see. With customary twenty-twenty hindsight, she saw it so clearly she even understood that from the innocent things she had said, Jon would think her privy to a private joke.

A week before Karon could have accepted the truth about Jon's family without a flicker of despair. Now it was the last straw. It was like a sick, perverted joke to learn she was a black market baby only to discover Jon was born with a silver spoon in his mouth.

''Maybe you had better tell me what your parents are like so I'll know what to expect,'' Karon said in a bleak voice.

Relieved to shift to familiar territory, Jon gave a thumbnail sketch of his father, adding little

Karon didn't already know from newspaper accounts.

"He's a great guy. If Dad was disappointed when I didn't go into the family business, he never showed it, and he spared me guilt."

"Very admirable. He must be proud of you. And. . .your mother?"

Jon sighed. "You've undoubtedly got some ideas about my mother. Most of them are the inaccurate impressions of strangers that she's a snob. You'll like her once the ice gets broken. If she's reserved around newspaper people, it may be because over the years they've given her good reason to be. Some misconstrue shyness for snobbishness. Mother is shy, except in two areas. One, when she's dealing with charities and asking for help on behalf of people not as fortunate as we have been. The other, genealogy. When she's following up a clue in hopes of adding another ancestor to the family tree, well, I'm afraid she can rival Midge for being brazen and bold. Don't be offended if Mother gives you a grilling."

"Grilling?" Karon gulped.

Jon shrugged with an accepting air. "No one is safe from her questions, love. Mother is always on the lookout for a long, lost relative, or someone who might be kin to someone she knows who is doing a family history."

"I suppose she finds it interesting." Jon

missed the forlorn lilt in Karon's voice.

"Very much so! It started as a hobby, but it's become a passion. The Wingate line is impressive . . . if I do say so myself."

"You may as well say it. Everyone else has." This time Jon didn't miss the grim line that formed at the corners of Karon's mouth and settled in to stay.

"Does it bother you? I was only teasing."

"No," Karon lied.

"It's interesting to know your ancestors," Jon explained. "Their names. Their accomplishments. What they did with their lives. Who we are at this very instant, Karon, was, to some extent, shaped by the countless generations before us, each of whom may have contributed a trait that creates a facet in our personaltiy. It's awesome when you think about it."

"I suppose," Karon agreed, as she tried to think of a way to steer the conversation away from family lines. "But I have heard it said if you give your family tree a good shake you risk having nuts fall out."

"Bite your tongue!" Jon ordered, laughing. "If you know what's good for you, you won't dare repeat that around my mother!"

"Has your mother ever found any nuts in the Wingate tree?"

Jon's smile deepened. His eyes twinkled. "If she had, she wouldn't tell a soul. I'm not sure

I would either. After all, we are *the* Wingates, my dear, and we have an image to maintain!"

"I'll try very hard not to embarrass you," Karon said, and Jon accepted the statement as a joke.

"Not to worry," he replied. "I told Mother to tell the maid to skip putting a pea under your mattress. I vouched you're a true princess."

"Better a pea under the mattress than a lot of questions I can't answer," Karon sighed. "My family wasn't much on close ties. I never even knew my grandparents."

"Oh, that won't stop Mother," Jon warned. "She'll view it as a challenge to figure it all out for you. Especially since she knows how much you mean to me."

Karon settled in for the remainder of the ride and knotted her hands together until her knuckles were white from the strain. If Althea Wingate was the bloodhound of bluebloods, Karon hoped that if she poked relentlessly into Karon's past, she would discover decent people. A family Karon would not be ashamed to claim.

Karon tried to be optimistic about the meeting only minutes into her future. But sodden reality kept pulling her back toward the dark, secretive past, peopled by faceless, nameless strangers whose genetic influence shaped her at present, and promised to form her future.

A future with...or without...Jonathan

Wingate. A decision she had yet to make.

Karon sensed the visit to Jon's parents was symbolic. She suspected he wanted her for his wife. Jon was waiting for his family to pass judgment on her. Karon decided Midge was probably right; the Wingates would approve.

But would they approve if they knew the truth? Would Jon be about to ask her to be his wife if he were aware of her beginnings as a black market baby of dubious lineage? Bought, sold! Born not of love, but possessed for a price?

Karon knew she could never marry Jon and carry her dark secret to the altar of his God, then live in fear her deceit would come to light to shatter her world. Nor could she tell Jon the truth after he proposed, because he would fervently assure her it made no difference. Jon was an honorable man. One who wouldn't go back on his word or shirk a commitment. Karon wanted Jon's love. . . but never his pity. There seemed only one solution—keep Jon from asking her the question she sensed was not far from his mind or hers. Karon hoped he wouldn't pop the question and want an answer before she knew it and was prepared to give it.

And to find the answer which would unlock her future, Karon realized she would have to discover her past.

# Chapter Three

"We're here," Jon said.

He pressed a button under the dash and majestic wrought iron gates swung open to allow them entrance to the private Wingate compound.

Karon felt a compelling urge to flee before it was too late and the situation grew out of her control. She wanted to leave while Jon and his love could remain a warm dream—before she chanced it becoming a chilling nightmare.

"Everything's going to be fine," Jon reassured and took Karon's hand as they walked up the wide flagstone path to the double doors that loomed ahead, ready for Karon's entrance to the wealthy world of the Wingates. "My parents are nice people—good Christian people. You have no need to fear them."

Karon knew Jonathan meant it as a reassurance. Instead she recoiled at the word . . . Christian. It shook her confidence further and served as a grim reminder of yet another area where she and Jon were worlds apart.

Jon pressed the door button. An instant later his mother appeared. Karon swallowed hard and came face to face with the socially conscious, formidable Althea—Pepper—Wingate, who regarded her with cool, curious gray eyes.

"Mother, my friend, Karon Kirlin. Karon, I'd like you to meet my mother, Althea . . ."

Karon made polite murmurings to Mrs. Wingate's welcome. She was hardly aware of what she said, or how often she smiled, but judging by the happy look on Jon's face, Karon decided her behavior was acceptable.

Warren Wingate—Buck, as he heartily instructed Karon to call him—returned from a trip on the lake in the family launch, and was as welcoming as his wife seemed somewhat detached.

"I'll take you to your room," Jon said. "So you can rest a bit and unpack."

"We'll be dining at eight," Althea announced. "With the Altmans."

Jon showed Karon to her room, then left her in privacy. Karon unpacked, touched up her makeup, then went downstairs in search of Jon.

He came in through a side door, accompanied by a woman who, from the strong family resemblance, Karon judged to be his older sister, Liz.

At the sight of Liz, Karon's heart sank. Elizabeth Wingate-Stephens was everything Karon was not. Liz was tall, tanned, perfectly coiffed, sophisticated, sleek, and wore her expensive jewels with the ease a teenager would wear dime store baubles.

"Liz, come meet my girl, Karon," Jon said. He drew Karon to them and the two women shook hands. "Karon this is my sister, Liz. Lady Elizabeth Wingate-Stephens. Her husband, Roderick, had to remain in London on business, and my niece and nephew are at summer camp, so Liz came alone to visit."

"*Lady?*" Karon's shocked question erupted.

Jon gave her a puzzled look. "Yes. . . Lady Elizabeth. But she's Liz to us. I thought I had told you. Liz married a titled Englishman. Roderick's an international lawyer."

"I'm just plain Liz when I'm in the States," Jon's sister emphasized. "No one calls me Lady, here. It would make me feel like someone's pet poodle!"

The three made small talk with Karon answering questions about her job and interests. Soon they were joined by Althea Wingate, who smiled hesitantly at Karon, took part in the conversation for a few minutes, and then excused herself again.

Liz glanced at her watch. "I must be getting dressed for dinner," she announced. Liz glanced at Jon, then at Karon. "Did Mother tell you we're entertaining tonight so it will be formal dress?"

"No, she didn't," Jon said smoothly. "But I was about to suggest it was time to dress for dinner." Karon glanced at Jon and he saw the uncertainty in her eyes. "Any dress you have will do," he murmured. "I'm going to my room and get into something suitable."

Karon went up the winding staircase to her room. She felt herself dizzy from the changes. In Chicago Jon was so casual. But in his parents' wealthy world, even at their summer home, which she had expected to have a casual air, he fit in with natural correctness.

She looked through her outfits hanging in the closet of the guest room and frowned. She hoped her good dress would do. She didn't want to embarrass Jon before his family and their friends.

Five minutes later Karon slid the zipper up and patted her dress into place when she heard a rap at the door. She expected it was Jon.

"Come in. I'm decent," she said.

The door opened to reveal Lady Liz in an expensive designer original.

"I'm not disturbing you?" Liz smiled warmly.

"Of course not," Karon said, and hastily plucked up her discarded clothes to bring order to the room. Liz stepped in, closed the door, crossed to the bed, and sat down uninvited.

"So you're Jon's girl," she murmured and her smile widened. "We've all been dying of curiosity. We knew he had someone he was serious about. Jon surely kept you tucked away in Chicago long enough! We were beginning to wonder if he was *ever* going to bring you to meet us."

"Oh really?" Karon said, nervously laughing.

"Jon's at the age where everyone expects him to marry and settle down."

"At the moment I think Jon's married to his work," Karon said.

Liz gave a ladylike frown. "Well, maybe that will change...when Jon meets the right girl."

"No one should take him from his work," Karon said carefully, to turn the conversation away from the direction it was taking. "He's truly talented. I'm sure that you're familiar with some of the buildings he has designed in Chicago and elsewhere."

"I've seen pictures," Liz admitted. "Jon designed this house."

"I didn't know that!"

Liz nodded. "It was his first project," she said. "Quite a masterpiece for a person so young. Perhaps that's what convinced Dad that he may as well give in and let Jon become an architect rather than expect him to step into the family business.''

The two women chatted idly, and Karon was relieved when she artfully managed to turn the conversation away from her own world, and got Elizabeth Wingate-Stephens to speak about her own fairytale existence in London.

''I must be going,'' Liz said when she heard Jon's voice downstairs.

''I'll be down shortly,'' Karon said.

Karon went to the door with the taller woman. She closed the door and it clicked shut, but not before Karon heard Liz hiss at Jon who was coming up the curved staircase.

''Psssttt! Jon! come into my room for a moment. I simply *must* talk to you *now* while I have a chance!''

Jon muttered something incomprehensible.

''No! It most certainly will *not* wait!'' Lady Liz said sharply, in a tone that signaled she might be used to issuing commands and having them obeyed at once. ''This time I'm not going to leave you to your own devices to decide something so important. I don't want Mother, Dad, the entire family, to be disappointed in how this is handled. Jon, you may not realize it yet, but it's truly a milestone.''

''Will you ever stop treating me like a little boy, Sis?'' Jon asked. ''Good grief—I know what I want to do! You act like I have no taste.''

Liz laughed lightly. "Oh, but I'm sure you do. Your designs express that. This is different, and more of my forte, so I want you to at least consider what I have to say before you barge ahead with impetuous plans of your own. I know Roderick would back me on this issue, and you've always respected his advice. Rod's quite a man of the world, you know. He usually sees situations for what they really are. Now be a dear and come to my room so we can discuss this in privacy and not worry about others listening in!"

Karon shrank inside. She leaned against the cool wooden door for support and her heart hammered wildly.

So! Lady Elizabeth Wingate-Stephens had come to her room, all charm and warmth, with the express intent of disarming her. Liz's friendly chatter had been created with the hope that from Karon's lips would come all the ammunition she would need to shoot down any plans Jon had of asking Karon to enter the Wingate family as his wife.

Liz was wasting no time about it, Karon thought bitterly. But then, Lady Liz had no time to waste. She was due to leave Sunday afternoon from O'Hare International Airport in Chicago for her flight to London.

Karon sat at the vanity table and mechanically touched up her makeup again. She could well imagine the run of conversation in Liz's room several doors down. Liz pointing out Karon's drawbacks. Jon stoically defending her. . . .

Karon felt devastated when she left her room, but she was thankful it wasn't apparent to the others when she joined them for dinner. Jon's face was unreadable following his private conference with Liz. But did Jon's hand on her arm seem more possessive? Were his eyes almost defiant? Was there a stubborn set to his jaw? Or was it all seen through her haze of suspicion?

The Altmans, a family as wealty as the Wingates, who had a summer home nearby, arrived. Karon was introduced around. She shrank inwardly when she became aware of the way Mr. and Mrs. Altman carefully looked her over, seeming to make note of every detail, before they exchanged a quick glance that seemed to say, "So this is the woman that Jonathan has chosen to marry!"

Karon hardly remembered the small talk as everyone adjourned to the formal dining room to be seated. Everything was a blur.

"Karon. . ."

She was harldy aware of her name being spoken. Karon glanced up, momentarily disoriented by the heaviness of her private thoughts. Karon faced Althea Wingate's expectant smile. Nervously Mrs. Wingate fingered the pearls at her throat. She seemed to be waiting for an answer to a question that Karon, in her confusion, had not even heard.

"Pardon me?" Karon murmured. Her face flushed hotly.

"Would you do us the honor of asking the Lord's blessing on us and our food, dear?"

Terror clutched Karon's heart. Her mind went blank. She couldn't even remember the short, rhyming table grace the Kirlin family had said on special occasions—Thanksgiving, Christmas, Easter. Seconds dragged out to eternity. Karon stared at her plate, helplessly horrified with humiliation. Jon's hand tenderly sought hers beneath the crisp linen tablecloth.

"Please, let me, Mother," Jon offered smoothly.

Before anyone had a chance to say otherwise, Jon offered thanks for their chance to fellowship and take food together.

Karon stared at her folded hands a long moment after she knew the others had raised their bowed heads. She burned with shame, which quickly gave way to smoldering anger. Furious thoughts centered on Althea Wingate, the person who had mercilessly put her on the spot by asking her to pray in front of them all.

After passing the bowl of mashed potatoes to Jon, Karon stole a glance at Althea Wingate. The socialite was looking elsewhere. Karon studied her face. There seemed no guile in her eyes. Or was Althea merely a clever and scheming actress as Liz seemed to be? Had it been a cheap shot? A subtle way to point out that the girl Jon had brought home didn't belong in their world? Or was it a message to Karon that if she entertained any ideas of accepting a place in the Wingate family she had better learn how to pray?

"What?" Karon asked, yanked from her simmering thoughts when Jon spoke. He was forced to repeat himself.

"I asked if you'd like some more roast, darling. It's delicious."

"No...I'm not very hungry."

"So I'd noticed," Jon murmured.

Karon forced a lame smile in answer to his, but she continued to shift the food around on her plate instead of eating. Karon had no hope of enjoying the food as tightly knotted as her stomach was with battling emotions.

"We'll have coffee in the living room," Althea Wingate instructed the maid. She led the way into the large, comfortable, expensively furnished room.

The Wisconsin air was chilly, typical early June weather, Warren Wingate said. With Jon's help the men lit a roaring fire in the massive fieldstone hearth.

Conversation, like the atmosphere, warmed around the fireplace as the logs snapped and cracked as flames licked higher. Karon saw the loving approval in Jon's eyes when she ventured to take part in the conversation and felt heartened.

It was after ten when the Altmans left. Buck Wingate bid the others good night. Liz followed suit. Althea assured her husband she would join him shortly.

"I think I'll stay up for awhile. Maybe take a walk on the beach. There's a beautiful full moon tonight." Jon gave Karon an obvious look of invitation.

"That sounds pleasant," Karon said.

"It's a splendid night for a moonlit walk on the beach," Althea agreed.

Jon smiled. "Care to come along, Mother?"

"Goodness, no!" Althea flushed, laughing. "I was young once, Jonathan Wingate. If you'll remember, two's company, and three makes a crowd. You and Karon go for your walk."

"I'll change into jeans," Karon said.

She crossed to the staircase and left Jon alone with his mother.

"I'll leave the patio lights on," Althea said. "And the door unlatched."

"We won't be too late," Jon promised.

"I'll see you both in the morning. Breakfast is at eight."

"We'll be up in plenty of time." Jon answered as Karon reappeared. "Good night, Mom."

*   *   *

The first real moment of happiness Karon had known that day arrived when Jon put his arm around her and they walked barefoot on the beach. Jon rolled up his trouser legs and they waded in the cool water, then walked once more on the shifting beach sand that was still warm.

"Look at the stars..." Jon said, his voice soft with awe. "A night like this really makes me aware of the One who made all." Jon sat on the wooden pier that jutted from Wingate property into the lake. He dangled his feet in the tepid water. Karon sat down beside him.

It was spectacular, the scenery breathtakingly beautiful the way the moon cut a ribbon of silver across the dark placid water, stars twinkled in the velvety sky, and thick pines were silhouetted, releasing a pungent scent that filled the air.

Jon put his arm around Karon and drew her head to his shoulder. He brushed a light kiss across her forehead. Karon turned to him and his lips dropped to claim her mouth.

"Oh...Karon," he murmured huskily.

Jon twisted to embrace her and his arms

encircled her waist. He pressed her softness against him. Jon's breath quickened at the contact. Karon's lips parted for his kiss. Jon's cologne enveloped her in its heady scent, and she felt weak and dizzy from the romantic perfection of the night and Jon's tender closeness.

Karon swayed, and she felt herself falling, falling, but Jon's lips never left hers. Karon's slim arms encircled his broad shoulders and her fingertips trailed playfully through the short hairs at the nape of his neck.

"Karon, you don't know what you're doing to me," Jon whispered, shuddering momentarily, before his lips longingly returned for more. Karon moaned softly when his lips trailed to the tender skin at the hollow of her neck, and Jon's masculine cheeks rubbed abrasively, pleasantly, against her silken, sensitive skin.

"Karon. . .Karon. . ." Jon's voice was a tender whisper. Jon's strong, supple hands cupped Karon's face. His eyes, dark and luminous in the moonlight, probed her gaze that was riveted on his. "You can't know the effect you have on me," Jon whispered in a dazed tone. "I've never felt for another woman all that I do for you."

Then, like a man possessed, unable to help himself or resist, Jon's lips fell back to Karon's mouth. The force of his kisses seemed to almost bruise Karon's tender lips. Karon felt herself drifting away from reality, captured, swept on by an eddying tide of desire.

Karon sighed softly with contentment as Jon rained kisses over her face and she brought his lips to hers once more.

"Oh. . .Karon. . ." Jon shivered.

With a movement that shocked Karon, Jon seemed to forcefully rip himself from her embrace. Hunching forward as he stared at the water riffling against the timbers of the dock, Jon gasped for breath. His profile was strangely stony. Jon was silent. Karon stared at him and felt vaguely hurt. Jon had gone from being so loving and adoring to. . .this! Karon worried that Jon was somehow angry with her.

She reached out to him. "Jon?" Karon whispered. "What's wrong? What did I do wrong?"

Jon seemed to flick her touch away with a shrug of his shoulder. She dropped her hand to the rough planking. Jon faced her in the moonlight. He gave her a crooked smile.

"You didn't do anything wrong," he said shortly. "If anything, you do too many things right. Please don't make it any harder on me than it already is," he implored in a soft, hoarse voice. "God knows how much I want you right now. So much I can hardly stand it. But I won't ever take you, Karon, not until it's right for us. What I feel for you, and what I hope you feel for me. . .well, that kind of enjoyment is a precious gift. I won't sully it by using it wrongly." Jon glanced away from Karon. "Right now," he sighed, "I want you so much it's like a dull ache all over me. Because I love you so much, I want what's best for you...for us."

"Jon, I don't know what to say," Karon whispered.

"Maybe waiting will make the possession even sweeter," Jon murmured. Shakily he arose and helped Karon to her feet. He took her hand and led her from the dock. "Let's go," he suggested in a soft voice. "Before I change my mind and beg you to stay. After all...I'm only a man."

\* \* \*

Back at the house Jon turned out the lights and locked the door. He kissed Karon one more time before they went to their rooms. In her luxurious quarters, Karon undressed and readied for bed. Her pulse quickened each time she remembered the way Jon kissed her, the way it made her feel, and how he had reacted. The special way he had explained his yearnings had proved he loved her, with far more conviction than if he had begged her to give in to their desires.

Karon recalled and cherished the things Jon had said. How different his ideas were! Instead of telling her that it was normal, assuring her it was natural, and seeking to convince her it was right for them to experience each other—healthy even!—Jon had stopped them from sharing the ultimate expression of love, for her sake, for his, protecting her and her gift of self that he someday hoped would be his.

Karon stared at the ceiling, wide awake, as her thoughts swirled when she recalled Jon's fervent explanations on the walk back to the house; that even when he was a child, his family had prayed for the girl who would someday be the chosen wife for him.

Karon shivered from the awesome realization. Imagine! The Wingates, immersed in family prayer, asking their Lord to guide, protect, and keep pure, a nameless, faceless woman who would one day become Jonathan Wingate's mate when the Lord brought them together and they recognized His will. They prayed also for Jonathan to remain strong, and pure in his love, in anticipation of the day he would approach the altar to claim the chosen woman as his wife, and as the Creator had planned the two would become one.

Karon realized Jon believed her to be that woman. The one meant for him. But was she?

Karon remained untouched, when many of her friends had made use of intimacy. Had it been because this God of Jon's had protected her? Or had it merely been personal happenstance? Or lack of an appealing enough opportunity?

Confusing but thrilling thoughts overshadowed Karon when she realized how much she meant to Jon. The warm, bright image paled and cooled when she remembered the crippling, shameful evidence in the strongbox back in her apartment.

Jon wanted her. But would he want her if he knew the truth? Karon tried to think it through. But the more she sought answers, the more needling the questions in her mind became. Her head seemed to almost ache from the effort of trying to reach conclusions.

Finally, unable to sleep, after what seemed like hours of lying awake, Karon slipped into her robe and slippers. She quietly undid the latch to the French doors that opened onto the balcony. Her eyes adjusted to the night and she crossed to a white patio chair. Karon had no idea she was not alone until Althea Wingate's low voice came from the nearby darkness.

"Can't you sleep either, dear?"

Karon wished she had stayed in her room!
"N-no."

"Probably for one of the same reasons I can't," Althea said sighing, and her voice drew closer. Althea took a seat beside Karon, and reached for the younger woman's hand. "I'm terribly sorry about what happened tonight at dinner. Truly, Karon, I never meant to embarrass you." Karon's cheeks heated at the memory. "It's always been a point to honor our special guest by asking them to say the table blessing."

Karon nodded. "I see," she murmured stiffly.

"I'm very sorry," Althea repeated. "When Jon said he was bringing a girl home . . . well, it was foolish of me, I realize, but, I'm afraid I . . . assumed . . . you were a committed Christian."

Karon glanced at her. Confusion swirled in her mind. As far as Karon knew, she *was* a Christian. At least that's the religious affiliation she selected when various forms demanded to know her race, gender, religious preference, and other personal statistics.

But Christianity, it seemed, as the Wingates knew and practiced it, was different from what it meant to Karon and the people she was accustomed to being around.

The Wingates were people who lived by a set of Biblical principles that had strong bearing on their way of thinking, behaving, living. Most people that Karon knew were like herself. They belived in God, but they didn't bother Him with prayers except in dire emergencies. They didn't have open Bibles around the house. And they didn't make a point of daily Scripture reading. Sometimes they went to services on Sunday if it was convenient, but they didn't get upset if there were more important things to take care of on Sunday morning.

Religion, as Karon knew it, meant that you didn't bother witnessing your faith to others. Karon had always been content to live-and-let-live. She feared that the Wingates were not.

In the past Jon had remarked how grateful he was to come from a strong, Christian home. Karon hadn't realized until that night how very much a part of his life Christ was. Christian teachings seemed to touch every facet of Jon's life . . . and love.

"Forgive me if I've hurt you," Althea requested softly. "Good night, dear." Then she was gone.

Karon remained on the balcony listening to the soft eternal swish of the waves that rhythmically slapped against the sandy shoreline. Memories from the past and present flooded forward to engulf Karon. Her heart swelled with such love that it evolved to become an ache that made her feel as if her heart would break in two.

Jon loved her. She loved him. But Karon knew the love they had was simply not enough. He wanted her. She wanted him. But love and desire were not enough. Many things drew them together. But as many things—very important things—drove them apart.

Karon was positive Jon's mother knew that.

Surely his sister Liz was aware of it. In a moment of illuminating truth, Karon had no choice but admit it. Jon, in time, would come to realize it, too. And if he did not, his family would force him to confront the visions they held. After all, they loved him and wanted the best for him.

In her heart Karon had to admit the painful truth: She was not the woman suited for a man like Jon Wingate. She suspected she was not the woman chosen for him by God. The woman they had prayed for so many times, waited for, longed to welcome into their family fold.

Somewhere that wonderful woman awaited Jonathan, no doubt praying for him as he prayed for her, living each day in joyful hope that with the heralding dawn would come the day when she would meet the man meant for her, chosen for her since the very beginning of time.

If she could just make it through the weekend, Karon decided, she would somehow find a way to break things off with Jon so he didn't waste any further time with her when he was meant for another.

It would break her heart, but Karon knew she had to part with Jon before she could suffer further pain and hurt under the realization that she was not the woman for him. She would end the relationship with Jon, before he came face to face with the knowledge that she was not the woman he waited for. He would try to let her down...gently...as a compassionate, Christian man like Jon would certainly try to do.

Even as Karon made her decision, and knew it was the right one for her, her heart ached with loss. Worse, she was already jealous of the woman, the good Christian woman, waiting somewhere, who would claim Jon as her own, and bring her gift of purity to his altar, and present it to him, as Jonathan Wingate would give her all that he was, all that he would ever be, forever.

Obviously, Jon was not the man for her, Karon comforted herself. But if there was a chosen woman for Jon, then somewhere, somewhere, there was the perfect man for her. And someday, Karon vowed, she would find him.

But first she had to find herself....

# Chapter Four

Sunday afternoon, although it wasn't apparent to the Wingates, Karon grew impatient to leave the luxurious, secluded summer home and return to her familiar niche in Chicago.

Before Liz left for O'Hare International Airport for the flight home, she said good-bye to her family. She hugged Karon, parting with such sincere words, that Karon momentarily doubted that Lady Elizabeth Wingate-Stephens disliked her and viewed her as an unsuitable match for her brother.

At three o'clock Karon took comfort from the thought that she and Jon would have to begin the drive back to Chicago soon. Karon brought her bags downstairs so she would be ready to leave as soon as Jon returned from a jaunt on the lake with his father. Karon sat on the front patio to wait.

Mrs. Wingate was busy returning calls that had been recorded on the answering machine while everyone was at church. Karon was so involved in her thoughts that she wasn't aware of Althea Wingate's approach. She jumped, startled, when the older woman spoke.

"By the way," Althea began, taking a seat near Karon. "I've been so busy it's slipped my mind, but I've been meaning to ask if you might be related to the Kirlins from the Boston area."

Karon tensed. The moment of truth Jonathan had warned about had just arrived. Karon stared straight ahead so Mrs. Wingate couldn't search her eyes.

"Mmmmm. . . I really couldn't tell you if I am or not," Karon replied in a casual voice. "I know little—in fact, really—*nothing* about my ancestors. My mother and father are dead. I never knew my grandparents."

Karon hoped the finality in her voice would get the subject dropped. It did not.

"That's a pity," Mrs. Wingate murmured. "It's so sad when knowledge of a family line becomes lost. I believe everyone should keep family records to be passed down to upcoming generations. Really, genealogies are fascinating.

The Bible is full of them. I know I appreciate the Scriptural genealogies more since I've become involved in that type of interest myself.''

''I'm sure you do,'' Karon said quietly.

A soft smile came to Althea's face as she gazed out at the whitecaps highlighting the deep blue swells on the lake. She gave Karon a quick glance.

''Sometimes we get so caught up with the present moment, and with our worries for the future, that we don't take time to pay respect to the past.'' Althea's eyes sought Karon's. ''I'm sorry . . . I'm probably boring you to tears. Until Jonathan got me started researching the Wingate lineage, I thought family trees were dull and a tremendous waste of time.''

''*Jon?!*''

Karon's heart momentarily stopped beating. An unnerving weakness tingled through her. Jon's responsibility for his mother's hobby was something Karon hadn't known. The news hit her with stunning force. Karon turned away as tears burned to her eyes.

So! Jon had pretended to poke fun at his mother's genealogic ambitions and interests, but the truth was that the Wingate line meant a great deal to him, too!

Mrs. Wingate chuckled softly. ''Yes, I'm afraid we've all got Jon to blame.''

"Th-that's very interesting," Karon stammered in a stiff voice.

Karon meant she found it personally intriguing that Jon, of all people, was responsible for his mother's obsession. Althea Wingate accepted it as a statement of Karon's fascination with her hobby.

"Oh, indeed it is!" she said, warming. With no coaxing from Karon, Althea Wingate began sharing family anecdotes she had uncovered. Just as Jonathan had said, the lovely socialite lost all reserve when she spoke of her family's history. Althea's eyes sparkled, and rich laughter punctuated the amusing stories she shared about the long line of illustrious Wingate men and women.

"What an interesting, accomplished family," Karon said and managed a smile.

"I always tease Buck and Jon that behind every successful Wingate man has been a good Christian woman."

Karon stiffened. She didn't like the new direction the conversation was taking again, but she felt helpless to change the subject without being rude.

"It's really too bad you don't know your roots," Althea said. "With your parents both gone, and no living relatives, it does make discovering the answers more difficult," she mused.

Karon said nothing. Althea fell silent and
looked out over the lake. Mrs. Wingate's eyes
became dreamy and faraway. Her voice, when
she finally spoke, was faint, scarcely more than
a whisper. Karon wasn't sure if Mrs. Wingate
was addressing her, or was giving voice to inner
thoughts.

"It's . . . sad . . . painful . . . not knowing where
your roots lie." Althea turned to Karon, suddenly including her in the fervent words. "If
you can, Karon, you really *should* do something about it! Find out who your family really
is."

Karon's lips parted with shock. She cringed
inside and miserably stared into Mrs. Wingate's
eyes. Feeling naked, ashamed, and helpless, as
if every dark secret from her past was revealed
to Althea Wingate's knowing gaze.

Karon lifted her chin in a flash of defiant
determination. It was ridiculous to think Althea
Wingate already knew her secret. She had no
way of knowing! Surely Jon's mother was
speaking in generalities—not specifics.

"I'm afraid I really wouldn't know where to
start," Karon murmured.

Mrs. Wingate shrugged. "You start with what
you know," she explained. "With what you
already know as clues, you dig for facts you
don't know. When you find them you have that
much more information to guide you in figuring

out what still remains a mystery. When you discover that. . . you continue on from there. It's amazing what facts you can dig up if you have the motivation to do it and the discipline to stick to the task.''

''I'm sure that's true,'' Karon replied.

''I've helped many people research their genealogies,'' Althea said. ''Sometimes for legal reasons—finding missing heirs. Sometimes for medical reasons—when there's a hereditary problem. And, thank goodness, sometimes just for fun.''

''It must be satisfying to help others by sharing your knowledge.''

Althea nodded. ''It is fulfilling. Lately it's been all the rage to search for family roots. So we genealogy bugs are less rare than we used to be.''

''I've given a few thoughts to searching into my past,'' Karon admitted quietly.

Althea gave her an assessing glance. Her eyes twinkled. ''Really, Karon? I have some excellent materials to help you get started—if you're really serious.''

The vague idea that had begun forming in Karon's mind a week earlier pushed ahead. The one thing that had held her back was the feeling of utter helplessness. She didn't know how to start looking for her true past. Suddenly, Althea Wingate was offering her the key to unlock her past.

"I-I'd love to have anything you can spare."

Althea gave Karon such a searching look that she flushed.

"Don't you dare accept the booklets and papers if you don't really mean it!" Althea teasingly warned. "I don't want you showing interest in my passion just to score points with your boyfriend's mother who everyone knows is notoriously fond of the subject."

Karon managed a faint smile. "Really, Mrs. Wingate, I'd be grateful for anything you can spare. I-I was thinking about researching my roots even before Jon told me about your hobby."

Mrs. Wingate rose. She tucked a stray wisp of hair into place and patted Karon's shoulder as she gave her a special smile.

"I'll get the things right now," she promised. "I'm sure Jon will want to leave for Chicago as soon as he and Buck return."

Althea barely had time to collect the material before the two men returned and Jon suggested they leave.

Buck and Pepper Wingate extended such warm invitations for Karon to return—any time—that she felt pressed to make some kind of answer.

"Maybe I will. Thanks for having me visit for the weekend," Karon said carefully.

When she got into Jon's car, in her heart Karon sensed she would never be back. Never!

Karon was silent all the way to Chicago. Jon was too wrapped up in his own thoughts to notice. Grateful for the silence, Karon analyzed the weekend.

All totaled, she had enjoyed the voyage into the strange world of the wealthy Wingates. But the very bottom line remained that she was relieved to return to her own realm. A world that was vastly different from the one the Wingates knew—and would expect her to enter —if Jon asked her to be at his side always...as his wife...as a Wingate woman.

That could never be! Karon harshly reminded herself, recalling the virtuous litany of strong Christian Wingate women.

Once more the realization settled in and Karon knew that she was going to have to gracefully find a way to break things off with Jon. Soon! Before it was too late. Before the pain could become too much to bear. It would be best for Jon. And best for her. There were too many things they held in common, but in too many important areas she and Jon were... worlds apart.

"The weekend went well," Jon commented when he carried Karon's luggage up to her apartment and waited for her to unlock the door.

"It seemed to," she agreed.

They entered the quiet apartment. Jon made no preparations to leave right away. Reflectively he watched Karon, who seemed preoccupied with picking up some of Midge's clutter. Jon noticed the way Karon averted her eyes and seemed painfully intent on keeping herself busy. Something was wrong, but Jon didn't know what.

"My parents really liked you. So did Liz."

Karon gave Jon a quick, wooden smile, then glanced away again. "That's nice to know," she said in a pained voice.

Jon went to her. "I *was* glad they liked you," he whispered. He cupped his hands on Karon's slim shoulders and turned her to face him. Wordlessly Karon looked up into his eyes. She saw such love there that it was like a knife plunged into her heart, then cruelly twisted.

"Karon...Karon..." he murmured. Jon's finger traced the delicate line of her jaw as he lifted her lips to his. Jon's breath was soft and warm against her cheeks. His arms tightened, pressing her to him so snuggly that she could feel the beating of his heart close to her own.

The scent of Jon's cologne engulfed her, and she sank away to the thrilling demands of his kisses. Tenderly Jon's lips left hers to bestow a kiss on each closed eyelid, the tip of her nose, and then he pecked a trail of light kisses across her cheek to her throat. Jon inhaled her perfume, and his arms crushed her more tightly before his lips came to hers with fiery desire.

"I love you, Karon," Jon whispered. "How I love you!"

At one time his words would have made Karon the happiest woman alive. Now they added to her pain. They brought her worries spiraling back to the moment.

". . .Jon!"

Karon's protest came out a faint, strangled cry, and further words were muffled by the intensity of his kisses. Kisses Karon found herself helplessly answering with deep passion of her own.

Being so intimately in Jon's arms, while knowing in her heart it had to be the last time, made it a torment. Logically Karon knew she had to break it off, even as Jon embraced her soft body against his tall, angular frame.

"Marry me, Karon. I want you for my wife, darling. Always. . .and forever." Jon removed his lips only the fraction of an inch it took to allow him to speak. "Be mine."

Karon tensed. Jon felt her stiffen. Impatient for an answer, Jon's lips claimed hers again.

This time, shocked and vulnerable, Karon was

unable to lose herself in the haunting spell of the moment. She strained away from Jon. Karon pried her lips from his. She arched her back to stare into Jon's face that seemed to bear the features of a stranger. Karon's world spun crazily. She stared—he stared. Karon didn't know if the strange emotion welling inside was going to result in laughter or tears.

"Marry me, Karon..." Jon tenderly urged.

Karon looked away, lowering her eyes until the thick lashes shielded her gaze from Jon's scrutiny.

"Karon?" Jon whispered, confused. He forced her to face him. Jon accepted her teary eyes and silence for happy agreement that went beyond speech. "Say something!"

Karon gave Jon a bald stare. Then her face crumpled. She wrenched away. Numb, she drifted to the opposite side of the room and stared unseeing at the twinkling city spread like a dark jeweled carpet before her. Karon's shoulders heaved, her back stiffened, and she clenched her fingers in a desperate attempt to get a grip on her emotions. Karon swallowed silent sobs and tears, choking.

Hesitantly Jon went to her. "Karon...what's wrong?" She turned her ravaged face to him, and shook her head, unable to speak. Her hollow eyes begged understanding, then, a burst of defiance replaced that emotion, and when a tear spilled over, with a testy motion she flung it from her cheek with a flick of her fingers. She turned and glared at Jon. Shocked, the breath whistled from him as he waited for her to speak.

"I see. . ." Karon said in a low, cold voice that shook. "Since your parents and your darling sister passed favorable judgment on me, you've decided it's safe to ask me to marry you? You? One of *the* important Wingates!"

Jon's complexion blanched at the venom in her words.

"Karon! You don't know what you're saying!" he gasped.

Jon took another step toward her, but Karon backed away. Instinctively Jon reached for her, but he sensed he dared not touch her, and his hand fell limply to his side. Karon's eyes narrowed and her voice dropped to a slashing whisper.

"Or maybe they didn't approve," she suggested bitterly. "Was their verdict just the opposite, Jon? And you're being headstrong? Going against their wishes this time—just as you probably did when you refused to go into the family business?"

Jon's face grew pale underneath his tan. He shook his head, unbelieving. "Karon. . . Karon. . . what's wrong with you? Where did you get such ideas?"

Hurt and confusion glowed in Jon's eyes. When Karon cruelly threw his proposal back in his face, his shoulders sagged with weariness. Karon turned her back on him, blinking back more tears.

After she had blurted the hurtful words, she knew she was wrong. Wrong! But it was too late. Jon spoke before Karon could form an apology.

Jon shoved his hands in his pockets. His shoulders were squared, his voice calm.

"Of course I care what my family thinks of you," Jon admitted stiffly. "If you were the kind of person I thought my family couldn't approve of, I wouldn't have brought you home to start with. I'd probably never have asked you out at all. I liked and respected you. I knew my family could, too. And they did, Karon. I don't need their permission to love you. I don't need their permission to ask you to marry me. I don't need their permission. . . but I do want their blessing!"

"Jon, I'm . . ." Karon's words faded. More tears came, this time for the hurt she had heaped on Jon, not for her own pain. Jon touched her. He licked his lips and tried again.

"I love you, Karon. I want you for my wife. I want you to be a Wingate woman . . ."

Without waiting for an answer, Jon took her into his arms. Karon's unbidden lips raised, seeking, fumbling to cling to his and draw comfort from his kiss. A sob tore from her throat when she realized how futile it was. Grasping at straws. They couldn't blindly live moment by moment when the future and truth waited, only a heartbeat away, to destroy their love.

Karon couldn't marry Jon. She would fall short of being a special Wingate woman.

Jon was the first to end the bittersweet kiss. "I'm waiting for your answer," he murmured. Karon turned her face away, even as Jon held her captive in his embrace.

"I can't marry you, Jon," she whispered. She looked at him, her soft eyes beseeching. "I won't marry you."

Jon didn't miss the choice of words. "Can't? Won't? Why not?"

". . . Because. . ." she finally said. "Just because."

Stung, Jon released her. Dazed, he left her and stared out over the city. He didn't look at her again. Couldn't. The tension stretched between them until the air seemed to crackle. Karon stared at her white knuckles and wished more than anything that Jon would go. Just *go!*

Eventually Jon faced her. His eyes were frank, his voice calm.

"After all the water that's passed under

the bridge," he said quietly, "I feel as if you really do owe me some kind of reason. Or . . . do you have one?"

"Of-of course I do!"

"But you've no intention of sharing it with me?"

Silence hung in the air again.

"No."

Jon's heavy sigh ripped the stillness. "I know something has upset you. I'd have to be an insensitive clod not to be aware that lately you've been edgy, nervous, sad. I thought it was something beyond your control. I hoped you'd snap out of it. Now I have no choice but to conclude it's *me* who's making you miserable. That *I'm* the source of your unhappiness."

Karon swallowed hard. "The problem doesn't concern you, Jon," she whispered through numb lips.

He laughed bitterly and faced her. "I'm very sorry to hear that," he said softly. "I was fool enough to believe that your problems were my problems. In case you've forgotten, Karon, I love you. I care about you. I believed that you trusted me and loved me enough to open your heart to me and let me share the burdens you carry."

Karon flushed. "I-I do. I mean, I did, but . . ."

"But?" Jon coaxed. The word hauntingly

demanded she finish the thought. *"But?"* Jon repeated.

"Listen, Jon, don't pressure me, okay?" Karon's eyes flashed.

Jon shrugged, defeated. "You win. Forget I said anything." Worriedly Jon ran his fingers through his sun-streaked brown hair. He fished the keys to his Porsche from his pocket and headed for the door.

"Good-bye, Jon," Karon said in a lifeless voice that clearly expressed she never expected to see him again.

Stunned, Jon faced her. His eyes were hollow when they met her tear-filled gaze.

"It hurts me to see you like this, Karon. So confused. So unhappy. I'm your friend! Maybe I could help you if you'd only let me try." Karon stared at the floor and shook her head.

"No, Jon. It's no good."

"You don't want me involved," Jon plunged ahead. "That's your right. But I'd like you to know that no matter what your problem, you don't have to handle it by yourself. If you won't let me help, there's Someone more willing and better than I. Someone who cares about you. Someone who loves you, Karon, even more than I can love you. Whatever your problem, darling, the perfect answer is found in the Lord."

"A panacea!" Karon started to snap.

But the blurted words did not come, thank
goodness. Karon realized she had hurt Jon
enough as it was, by refusing his proposal, and
help, without refusing his God and dearest
beliefs as well.

"Keep it in mind," Jon suggested. "The Lord
is waiting to help you. But before God can
work a miracle in your life, sweetheart, you
have to step aside and ask Him to enter.
Turn your problems over to Him. The Lord will
guide you, and He'll never lead you wrong. I'll
pray for you. I'll try to get in touch later this
week."

The door clicked shut to signal Jon's departure. Karon raised her eyes and stared at the
closed door. She hadn't really understood what
he meant by his parting words but she was
relieved that he was gone.

Maybe Jon thought things would be better
later in the week. But he was wrong. And she
wouldn't be there later if he did try to contact
her. Furthermore, woe be unto Midge Harper
if Midge spilled the beans about Karon's
whereabouts after she was gone!

Grimly Karon made a list of things to attend
to before she left on vacation to find herself,
and if she were lucky, the information that
would help her discover the truth about her
real family. Only by exploring the past and
learning who Karon Kirlin really was, she

decided, could she hope to come to grips with everything, reconcile it in her mind, and chart a happy course in the vast, vast future that lay ahead.

A future *without* Jonathan Warren Wingate!

# Chapter Five

Monday evening Midge returned home to find Karon struggling up the stairs from the basement laundry room in the apartment comlex. Midge found nothing unusual in that until she followed Karon to the apartment and watched her refill suitcases she had emptied only the night before.

Midge stared at the busy blonde and counted to ten before she demanded an explanation. As moody as Karon had become, Midge really didn't hold much hope for an answer. When Karon explained she was going away to research her roots, Midge laughed at first. Then she stared, open-mouthed with shock when she realized it was true.

"That's the craziest thing I've heard all day!" Midge cried. She rolled her eyes and raked her fingers through her short crop of coppery hair. "What prompted the sudden interest in genealogy? And the sudden disinterest in Jon?"

Karon remained mute. Midge counted to ten again, remembered what her mother had told her about asking personal questions, then plunged ahead.

"I can't believe you're . . . running away like this." Midge chose her words carefully. "Tell me you're not leaving."

Karon glanced in Midge's direction and offered a thin smile.

"I won't tell you I'm not leaving because I just finished telling you I am." Karon emptied her lingerie drawer into the open suitcase.

"Why, Karon? Why, for crying out loud?"

Preoccupied with other things to think about, Karon chewed her lip and looked around to select things she would need.

"*Why*, Karon?" Midge reiterated. Her insistence broke through Karon's thoughts.

"Oh. Because. Just . . . because," Karon dismised. She turned back to her closet and hoped it would suffice for an answer.

"*Because* is a rotten, evasive excuse for a reason!" Midge pointed out. " You can do better than that!"

Karon laughed. She suddenly understood why Midge's feature stories were so pithy. People didn't stand a chance when pitted against Midge Harper. She could prod, goad, coax, and cajole answers until even the most impudent questions resulted in some kind of printable reaction.

"No comment!" Karon said lightly. "I plead the Fifth."

"Baloney!" Midge snorted. "You know what you're doing and why. I've outwaited others, Karon, I can wait you out."

Karon sighed. "Midge, it's the only answer I can give right now."

Midge shook her head. "Not the only answer you *can* talk about...the only one you *will* talk about." Midge crushed her cigarette out in the ceramic ashtray she carried whenever she went into Karon's room. She exhaled a stream of smoke when she spoke, studying Karon through the haze. Midge's features, dappled with freckles, softened with sympathy when she detected the nameless misery in Karon's eyes.

"You've been a shadow of yourself for over a week," Midge mentioned gently. "I've kept my nose out of your business, as you may have noticed, and I hope appreciated. I can't stand by any longer, Karon. I'm butting in! What the heck is going on with you? Tell me," Midge

warned with a grin, "before you force me to use
a few seldom called for tricks from the famous
Harper-Arm-Twist School-of-Journalism, guar-
anteed to get answers out of the most stoic
stonewallers. *Give!*"

And Karon did. More because of an over-
whelming need to talk to someone than because
of Midge's insistence.

"You want to know what's wrong? As of
now—*everything!*" Karon's gaze drifted to the
metal box beside her bed. Midge's eyes followed. "Have a look in that."

Midge picked up the strongbox. "What is
it?"

"Take a look and see," Karon casually in-
vited. She folded garments and tucked them into
spaces remaining in the suitcases. "It will save
me a lot of explaining."

Midge displayed uncharacteristic reluctance.
She gave Karon another glance to make doubly
sure it was all right, then gingerly opened the
box. Midge adjusted her reading glasses and
began examining the documents spread across
her lap. The longer she read the more amazed
her expression became. She didn't speak until
she replaced the papers in the box, locked it,
and set it on the floor.

"Karon...I can't believe it," Midge
whispered. Her voice was soft with horror.
Karon shrugged. Tears were close to the surface

again. "Karon, I'm terribly sorry." Karon nodded acceptance of Midge's sympathy. "No wonder you haven't been yourself," Midge mused.

A bitter smile came to Karon's lips. "It's rather hard to *be yourself* when you don't feel you even know who you really are."

"I can imagine that's true," Midge agreed.

"When I discovered the box, I thought in a few days I would be able to comprehend it, accept it, then forget it. I figured I could pick up the pieces of my life and go on as before. But Midge... I can't! So I've got to try to figure it all out."

"This search... it's so you can sort it out?"

Karon nodded. "My first impulse was to find out who I am—for Jon's sake. Now I'm realizing I must do it for my own good."

"Find out for Jon's sake? That doesn't make much sense. What does he have to do with it?"

"A lot, when you realize that Jon happens to be a Wingate, Midge. One of *the* Wingates."

Midge's mouth dropped open. "You're kidding!" she gasped.

"I wish I were."

Midge slapped her forehead with the heel of her hand and moaned sickly. Her face drained of color, then her cheeks glowed pink.

"Oh, Karon, I could bite off my tongue

when I remember all the things I've said to Jon!''

"Yes, Midge," Karon sighed. "The woman you told Jon Kitty swears is a notorious snob is his mother. And, as if that's not enough, Althea Wingate has a pet hobby—family trees— genealogy. There's not a *nobody* in the family. In fact, Jon's sister, Liz, married someone titled in London.''

"I could die," Midge groaned.

"So could I," Karon agreed. "Anyway, now you can see why someone with my background would never fit into the Wingate line. And religion's a sticky problem, too.''

Such a long silence followed that Karon realized, idly, it might be the first time in recorded history that the twenty-five-year-old reporter was speechless.

"You haven't told Jon this, have you?"

"Would you?" Karon answered Midge's question with one of her own.

Midge thought it over. "I don't know," she replied. "Probably not. But then Jonathan Wingate's not your average guy. I think he would understand.''

"I'm sure he would," Karon agreed dryly. "Jon's religious beliefs would leave him little choice. He would do the Christian thing, Midge. He would feel committed to me. Jon isn't one to shirk agreements or shrug off responsibilities.

I couldn't marry Jon, and then live on wondering if he married me because he felt sorry for me, and not for all the right reasons. I'll marry for love . . . but never for pity."

Midge quirked a brow. "You talk as if Jon proposed!" she cried.

Karon nodded. "He did. But I turned him down."

Midge moaned. "Any other girl would've accepted a proposal like that in a flash and worried about the future later. Golly, Karon, guys like Jon aren't a dime a dozen. Plus, he really loves you. If you don't marry him, time will pass, and some other girl will."

"I told you I wasn't going to marry him" Karon said sharply. "And I doubt he would want me if he knew the truth." Karon made a face. "Althea Wingate would probably send for her smelling salts if *she* knew. When it comes to genealogy, she's like a bloodhound on the trail. There would be no keeping things a secret. And when I marry, I want there to be no secrets. I'll tell the truth—and know that the man I marry loves me enough that it makes no difference."

"You think Jon's not that man?"

"That's just one of the things that pulls us apart, Midge. After the weekend I doubt that enough bridges exist to link our worlds."

"So my roommate, also known as Chicken

Little, instead of facing Jon with her problems, is going to run away?'' Midge's chiding tone was meant to needle Karon into other action. She purposely ignored the bait.

''That's right!'' Karon agreed lightly.

Midge sniffed. ''I can see you've made up your mind so I won't try to talk sense into your pretty head.'' The reporter lit another cigarette, shook out the match, dropped it into the ashtray, and got comfortable on the bed. ''Tell me what's on your agenda.''

Glad to leave personal issues behind, Karon filled Midge in on her travel plans that would take her to the Timberline Lodge, a resort in northern Minnesota, on a large lake. It was near the town where Karon suspected her roots lay, judging from the addresses on the old documents in the metal box.

''My boss agreed to let me use up a few weeks of vacation time I've accumulated. And a few more days if I really need it.'' Midge nodded. ''I made my reservations through the agency today. I plan to leave first thing in the morning.''

''You're not wasting any time, are you?''

Karon shook her head. ''I'll leave enough cash for you to take care of my share of the expenses.''

''I hope you're doing the right thing,'' Midge said.

''I hope so, too. . .''

"What about Jon?" Midge asked. "Does he know you're going away?"

"No."

Midge was thoughtful. "What should I tell him when he calls and you're not here?"

Karon's heart skipped a beat at the thought. "Tell him it's over between us. Tell him I died. Tell Jon anything you like, Midge, just don't you dare tell him the truth!"

"I can't do that to him!" Midge protested.

"Don't worry about it," Karon said. "You're creative, Midge. You'll think of something."

"What if Jon won't accept what I have to say for an answer? What if he contacts your boss?"

"No problem," Karon said glibly. "I swore Mr. Carruthers to secrecy. You've got to keep my secret, too, Midge. I know Jon would think he had a duty to find me—to try to help me solve my problems. He's that kind of guy. Trust me, Midge, it wouldn't help. It would only make things worse."

"Maybe not."

"Believe me, Midge, it would. Things are over between Jon and me. I've faced it. He'll have to. You'll have to, also. Jon and I happen to be two nice people who aren't meant to be together. So promise me you won't tell him where I am or why. Jon's showing up would only hurt me and prolong the pain. Promise?"

"Oh, I guess so," Midge reluctantly agreed.

Karon smiled. "Good. Now what do you say we get supper started?" Karon suggested.

"A terrific idea. In fact, that's the sanest thing you've said since I got home," Midge murmured.

\* \* \*

The next morning Karon was up at dawn, ate a quick breakfast with Midge, loaded her small yellow car for the trip, and was prepared to leave before Jon could even think of calling her at such an early hour.

"I'll leave now," Karon said as Midge got ready to go to work.

Midge gave Karon a solid hug. "Take care, friend."

"I will," Karon promised. "You have my number and the name of the resort?"

"On my desk."

"I'll keep in touch," Karon said.

"See that you do!" Midge warned. "You know that I wish you every good thing. Maybe in Minnesota you'll find it."

"I have to try," Karon whispered. "I'll see you soon."

With a smile far braver than she really felt, Karon slid into her car and switched on the ignition. Resting on the front seat in her attache case were the contents of the strongbox and the information Althea Wingate had generously shared with her to aid in her search.

With luck, the scant supply of clues would be enough to help Karon find the first answers to the series of riddles that plagued her. If she were determined and disciplined enough, she trusted the unsettling questions that hounded her day and night would be answered.

The world knew her as Karon Kirlin. Now the big question remained. Who was she . . . *really?*

# *Chapter Six*

**K**aron enjoyed the scenic drive across Wisconsin. She made steady progress through the Badger State, admiring the picturesque dairy farms that dotted the dells and rolling hills. Karon marveled at the thick pine forests that clung to the awesome outcroppings of jagged rock, and realized that the wide highway was an engineering accomplishment.

Karon was tired when she reached the bustling seaport city of Duluth, Minnesota's famous harbor, in time to catch rush-hour traffic. Other drivers soon left the road to seek shelter for the night. But Karon, who had a room awaiting her at the Timberline Lodge, continued, assured that within two hours she would arrive at her destination.

It was dusk when Karon slowed, peering to make out the names of the various resorts, wood-burned into large planks, erected at the edge of the highway. Bright arrows pointed turns to be taken.

When Karon saw the sign announcing the Timberline Lodge she flipped on her signal and turned onto the winding path that wended through thick evergreens and clumps of birch. Karon rounded a sharp bend in the trail and saw the resort building silhouetted against the still, glassy lake.

Welcoming lights glowed from the dining room that overlooked the sandy beach and tranquil lake. Wrought iron gaslights lined the sidewalks. A red neon light identified the lobby. The rustic Timberline Lodge sprawled along the lakefront, nestling up to the close forests that smelled of pine and mingled with the aroma of fresh water, warm sand, and the tangy odor of seaweed.

Karon nosed her car into an empty parking slot, locked the doors, slung the strap of her leather shoulder bag into place, smoothed her dress, and approached the lobby.

Karon nodded at the few guests waiting in the lobby when she entered the area. A few vacationers passing from the dining room greeted her with friendly smiles and continued on their way. The soft clank of cutlery against china and a hum of conversation floated from the eating area. Further away in the lounge, a dance combo played popular tunes with a lilting beat.

Karon approached the horseshoe-shaped counter and pressed the button to signal the desk clerk. An elderly man came out to assist her.

"May I help you, miss?" he inquired, adjusting his glasses. Karon smiled. "My name is Kirlin—Karon Kirlin—from Chicago. I have a reservation."

"One moment, please," the clerk excused himself and reached for the file box. Just then the switchboard lit up. "Excuse me," he apologized. "I'll be with you after I take this call."

Karon examined her fingernails and pretended not to listen to the clerk's conversation. Examining the furnishings and decor, she glanced to the dining room just in time to see a tall, dark-haired, well-dressed man leave the room. He halted, as if his eyes needed time to adjust to the different lighting, then his steel blue eyes met Karon's curious gaze.

The man quirked a dark brow and his eyes grew puzzled, almost quizzical, before his stare evolved to border on disbelief. His lips parted, and he seemed about to speak, then shocked, gently reached out to rest his fingertips on the wall as if to draw needed support. The man stared at Karon as if time stood still for him.

Karon's eyes were riveted on his. Her brow dipped into a frown at his unusual reaction. She suspected that he was going to say something to her. Instead, he came straight for her, then to her surprise, breezed by and entered the Timberline Lodge's private office without so much as a word or further glance in her direction.

Karon turned back to the desk clerk thinking the stranger's reaction was most unsettling. She idly wondered if at one time she had helped him make travel arrangements and he had remembered her face. Karon rejected the explanation as quickly as it had come to her. She knew she had never seen the man before. A face like his was unforgettable. Already she could close her eyes and picture him, detail for detail, his features branded into her memory.

"You say you have a reservation?" the desk clerk said, pulling Karon's attention back to the moment.

"Yes, the name is Kirlin. Karon Kirlin."

The clerk started to sort through the reservations. The intercommunications system buzzed sharply.

"Oh, fuss and bother!" he muttered, sighing. "Sorry, miss. Please excuse me again. This shouldn't take more than a minute." The clerk gave Karon a helpless smile before he disap-

peared into the inner office without bothering
to knock. He returned as quickly as he had left.

"Maybe now we can get you registered, Miss
Kirlin," he said and gave her a hopeful smile.
"Kirlin . . . Kirlin . . ." he whispered, thumbing
through the K's. Then he flipped back to the C's.
The clerk's scowl deepened. "We don't seem
to have a reservation in your name." To make
sure the clerk whisked through all the cards on
the chance it had been incorrectly filed.

Karon was exhausted. Her back ached. Her
eyes were gritty from the long drive in summer
sunlight. She was in no mood for trouble and
inconvenience. The "No Vacancy" sign now
lighted the marquee and winked an ominous
message through the large bay window.

"But you *must* have!" Karon insisted.

The clerk shook his head, "We don't. I'm very
sorry. Are you positive you made the reservation with the Timberline and not with another
resort with a similar name? People do tend to
make that kind of mistake."

Karon's nerves grated at the suggestion. "I am
a travel agent," she explained crisply. "I do happen to know how to go about booking and con-
firming reservations. I most certainly did *not*
make a mistake!"

"Then there must be some other error,"
the clerk persisted. "Usually it wouldn't be
a problem, miss, but there's no vacant room

available right now."

Karon had counted on a room. Being turned away, faced with the unpleasnat prospect of trying to find accommodations late at night, when summer travelers had probably rented every available room, made Karon's temper flare.

"It's not my fault. I had a confirmed reservation. This certainly isn't very good advertising. . ."

"I'm very sorry, miss," the clerk repeated. "I know you're tired and disappointed. You need a room. Let me try to find you one nearby. The Timberline will pick up the tab in order to compensate you for your trouble."

The clerk reached for the telephone on the desk and flipped the directory open. He began dialing. The clerk hadn't completed the sequence of numbers before the tall, dark-haired man emerged from his office. He glanced at Karon and detected the frustration on her features. He looked at the desk clerk and noticed his strained manner.

"Is there some kind of problem, James?" the man addressed the slight clerk.

The small man nodded his head. "We have a problem over a reservation, sir. The young woman claims she had a confirmed reservation but we have no record of it. Unfortunately, there are no rooms available. I suggest we solve the problem by finding her a room at one of the other resorts, if we can, and pick up the tab.''

Derek Eastwood nodded. He looked at Karon but spoke to his desk clerk. ''Maybe that won't be necessary, James. If Miss...'' Derek Eastwood fished for her name.

''Kirlin,'' Karon supplied.

He gave her a quick smile. ''If Miss Kirlin will agree, we can put her up in one of the guest suites of my home.'' He faced her. ''My private home is nearby. It adjoins Timberline property. You would be comfortable there, and of course, you would have access to all the resort has to offer.''

''Good idea, Mr. Eastwood,'' James said, his relief evident. ''Chances are that other resorts are booked to capacity, too.''

Karon shrank away from the idea and Derek seemed to sense it. His smile was amused. Laugh lines crinkled at the corners of his blue eyes.

''I can promise you all the privacy you hope for—if you decide you want it,'' he said. ''My staff is excellent. Please accept my hospitality, Miss Kirlin, at least for the night.'' Derek Eastwood touched her arm. An almost electric tingle rippled through her. Karon glanced into his eyes and saw that he had witnessed the reaction. She flushed, but he continued on as if he had not noticed.

''You're tired. What you need is rest—not hassle. Stay at my home tonight and I guarantee you the first room available at the lodge is yours... if you want it."

Karon glanced at her watch. What he offered was a pragmatic solution to her immediate problem.

"All right," she agreed. "And thank you."

"Think nothing of it," Derek Eastwood dismissed her words. "I trust you haven't eaten yet? When you finish your meal, Miss Kirlin, look me up in my office and I'll take you to my home."

With a curt glance at the silent desk clerk, and a friendly nod at Karon, the boss of the Timberline Lodge disappeared toward the lounge.

Karon stared after him and found herself hungry for another glimpse of his almost savage handsomeness.

Derek Eastwood sensed her eyes on him. Arrogantly he turned to confront her. His eyes met and locked for an extended moment before Karon modestly tore her gaze from his, stiffly turned away, and made her way into the almost deserted dining room as her pulse hammered wildly.

Forty minutes later, Karon left a tip on the table and passed into the lobby. She rapped lightly on Derek Eastwood's door. A chair creaked. Footsteps crossed the room. The door cracked open and Derek smiled down at her.

"I'll be right with you," he promised.

Karon lingered just outside the door of Derek Eastwood's private office in the shelter of a large potted plant. She waited only a few moments while Derek Eastwood locked file cabinets and brought order to the clutter on his desk. But it was all the time it took for her to witness a young man walk in from the parking lot, ask for a room, fill out a card, and without question, be issued a key. And with no mention of a prior reservation. Outside the bay window the "No Vacancy" sign no longer blinked!

Karon was about to confront the desk clerk to remind him she had been promised the first available room. But before she could, Derek Eastwood's forceful grip on her elbow rushed her through the door he held open, and guided her into the velvety, star-studded Minnesota night.

Derek slid into his white Lincoln. He backed from his slot, then waited for Karon to catch up. She followed behind him, braking when his red lights flared.

Karon felt as if she were a sleepwalker moving through a dream. It was so unreal! She could hardly believe she was so trustingly following a stranger to his private home. For a stark instant Karon wondered if she should turn and flee the situation. But before she could reach a decision, Derek swung into a parking space and she took one alongside, shoving aside the apprehension she felt. Derek Eastwood was a businessman. He was offering her a room—no more, no less—so she had no need to assess her own motives in accepting the gesture.

Derek helped Karon with her luggage and made polite conversation as he led her up the flagstone path to his luxurious home. He set her bags down in the foyer.

"Mrs. Sowder, my cook and housekeeper, will take you to the guest room," he promised.

"Cookie! I'm home," Derek called. "We have a guest."

A stout woman with tightly curled gray hair came from the kitchen. She was dressed in a navy blue uniform and her white apron was crisp and clean. At the sight of Karon the chubby woman's eyes, which had been warm, almost mirthful, chilled a degree. Mrs. Sowder murmured a polite welcome, but her troubled eyes expressed the truth her words did not dare. Karon was an intruder in Mrs. Sowder's household!

Karon hadn't missed the stare of surprise that had fallen on the housekeeper's jovial features, then flown to envelope Derek in a look of stern disapproval. In the face of Mrs. Sowder's countenance, Derek smiled and his blue eyes sparkled with an air of smug satisfaction.

Karon couldn't begin to imagine *why*.

Mrs. Sowder dourly led Karon to her quarters.

The sumptuous rooms were far superior to anything offered at the nearby Timberline Lodge, or anywhere else in the area, Karon was sure.

Deciding not to dwell on the puzzling events that had led to her arrival at Derek's home, nor the housekeeper's odd reaction, Karon snapped open her suitcase and put the matter from thought, promising herself there would be a room for her elsewhere in the morning.

As tired as Karon was, when she slipped between the pastel satin sheets, sleep evaded her. It was so odd. So very odd! The more Karon thought it over, the more it seemed as if Derek Eastwood *wanted* her in his private home.

But why?

No reason came to her. They were strangers. Yet he had instantly opened his home to her. And there was the young man, too, who had been issued a room without question. Why had she been denied quarters? Could it possibly be that somehow Derek Eastwood had engineered the scene that left her little choice but to accept his offer?

The idea that Derek Eastwood was attracted to her was a flattering thought. There was no denying that she was attracted to him. The thought that she appealed to Derek enough at first sight for him to do something about it gave Karon pause even as she savored the sweet knowledge that she was attractive.

Derek Eastwood, whatever else he was, already proved to be a man who took charge of every situation. He was unlike any man Karon had ever encountered. That realization both worried and delighted her.

For well over a week Karon found herself loathing to face another day and the grim emotions that haunted her. Derek Eastwood had miraculously changed all that. Karon found herself wishing for morning—when she would see Derek Eastwood again.

Maybe Derek was her destiny, Karon thought sleepily. Jon had said so many times that there was a master plan. A purpose for every life. Jon believed that nothing happened—either good or bad—but that God in His sovereign wisdom allowed it. Every little thing, Jon said, eventually served God's plan.

*Jon said!*

Karon's eyes flipped open in the darkness when she realized the tangled web of confusion yet in her thoughts. Here she was, she thought wryly, trying to forget Jon, wildly attracted to a handsome stranger, embarking on a vacation to forget her problems in general and Jonathan Wingate in particular. But while Jon was miles away in person, he was still as close as her most intimate thoughts—his love for her and his God haunting her.

Sighing, Karon punched the pillow and sank

her head into the dent. Then her thoughts left
Jon and centered on Midge Harper. A smile
came to Karon's face. Midge, who was as flirty
as she was frank changed boyfriends almost as
regularly as she turned calendar pages. The
reporter lived by the motto that the best way
to forget an old love was by discovering a new
one.

How strange Midge hadn't offered that solution to Karon when she had confided things
were over with Jon! Karon decided maybe
Midge hadn't furnished her favorite advice
because she knew that the memory of Jon, and
all he meant to Karon, wouldn't be a quick image to fade. It would take a long time to forget
Jonathan Wingate, Karon knew. But Derek
Eastwood, a man so handsome, so wealthy, so
urbane, so sophisticated and attractive, would no
doubt hurry the process along.

Karon sighed with happy anticipation and
glanced at her watch to count the hours until
the coming dawn. She would live up to Midge's
slogan. She would put her old love behind her.
Perhaps by discovering a new one: *Derek
Eastwood!*

# *Chapter Seven*

**S**unlight slanted across the bed to fall on Karon's face and she awakened. Rolling over, she opened one sleepy eye to consult her watch and decided to get up. She showered in the adjoining bathroom, dressed carefully, and quickly applied makeup before she ventured downstairs in hope of finding Derek Eastwood.

The boss of the Timberline Lodge had already departed. Karon hoped her disappointment was not evident when the housekeeper informed her he was gone for the day.

"Mr. Eastwood instructed me to give you a tour of the house," Mrs. Sowder informed her. "You may as well eat breakfast here rather than go to the lodge."

Without asking Karon's preference, the woman set a plate of sausage, eggs, and warm buttered toast before her, fetched a coffee cup and set the glass pot on a ceramic trivet.

As soon as Karon finished eating Mrs. Sowder reminded her of the ordered tour. Karon was about to express her opinion that it was a waste of time since she hoped to be moved to the Timberline Lodge by nightfall. But Mrs. Sowder's grim air silenced any protestation Karon was tempted to give.

The stolid housekeeper shepherded Karon from room to room. She found herself wishing Jon could view the home. With an architect's knowledge, he would have appreciated the tour far more than she.

By the time the tour of the downstairs was completed, Mrs. Sowder no longer seemed quite so stuffy and disapproving.

"The bedrooms are upstairs. Mr. Eastwood's. Yours. Victoria's. Mr. Eastwood told me to tell you that you have access to all his home has to offer—the library, the game room, the patio— everything."

*Victoria!*

So *that* was it! No wonder Mrs. Sowder was so disapproving. The knowledge Derek Eastwood was married almost brought Karon to tears as her tantalizing daydreams vanished, leaving behind an aching hollowness.

"Is Mrs. Eastwood involved with the resort?" Karon asked casually.

Mrs. Sowder glanced at Karon with alarm. "Mrs. Eastwood?" she repeated carefully. Relief seemed to flow into the woman's features when she understood what Karon meant. "Oh, Victoria's not Mrs. Eastwood. Miss Dawson is Mr. Eastwood's associate. Victoria stays here when they're in the area on business. She goes with Derek wherever company concerns take him."

"I see," Karon murmured.

And she did.

From the way Mrs. Sowder had spoken, Karon sensed that there was more to it than just a boss-secretary relationship. Even though Karon knew the jealousy she suffered was a stupid, useless, damaging emotion, she couldn't help the hurt she experienced with the realization that Derek Eastwood already cared for another woman. Karon sharply reminded herself she was nothing to him—a patron of his resort—nothing more. Anything she had thought of him were only foolish imaginings on her part.

"I can fix your meals here or you can dine at the lodge," Mrs. Sowder broke in on Karon's thoughts.

"I'll dine at the Timberline, thanks. I hope to move there as soon as a room is available."

"Very well." The agreeable words expressed

the housekeeper's relief.

Mrs. Sowder left for the kitchen and Karon returned to her suite long enough to get her papers and the materials Althea Wingate had given her.

The night before Karon stayed up long enough to look through the local telephone directory. She had been rewarded with the information that the Peterson Law Firm was still located at the same address as was given on the firm's letterhead from almost a quarter of a century before. Karon hoped that, if the lawyer who handled her proceedings wasn't still with the firm, a colleague might at least have some knowledge of the case or be willing to help.

A half an hour later Karon halted in the parking lot of the firm. The building was new. Carefully trimmed shrubs flanked the curved walk that passed an ornate water fountain, skirted by flower boxes brimming with petunias.

Karon hurried into the building, scarcely daring to hope she would be lucky enough to see an attorney. She planned only to ask for an appointment when the elderly receptionist listened to her sketchy story. The woman buzzed one of the lawyers, repeated the bare facts, then asked if someone could consult with Karon.

"Send her in. I'll fit her into my schedule," was the response.

The woman guided Karon down a short hallway. A door opened at the end of the corridor. A pleasant, sandy-haired man a few years older than Jon stepped out to greet her.

"Miss Kirlin?" He offered his handshake. "I'm Steven Peterson. Uncle Mathias founded the firm, but he's no longer involved. Maybe I can help you." He drew Karon into his office and gestured toward a chair.

Quickly Karon sketched in the story and spread the papers on the desk for his examination. He leaned back in his swivel chair, clasped his hands behind his head, and stared at the ceiling.

"Uncle Matt was afraid something like this would happen."

"What do you mean?"

The attorney sat ahead and toyed with his pen. "When I was just a child and my father was in the firm with Uncle Matt, I recall them having a falling out with one of the younger lawyers who had been taken on as a junior partner. They had to let the fellow go." Steven Peterson met Karon's eyes. "The attorney who handled your...placement...was not as ethical as one might wish. Fearing his shady dealings would land the entire firm in trouble, Uncle Matt had no choice but to terminate his association."

A feeling of hopelessness seeped over Karon. "Surely there are some kind of records!"

The attorney shrugged. "Somewhere, perhaps. But not here. Even if the attorney involved worked on your case on Uncle Matt's time and kept careful records, we probably couldn't produce them. Ten years ago the original office burned to the ground. Most of the files were destroyed, charred beyond salvaging.''

''There must be someone, something,'' Karon whispered doggedly. Her voice shook with disappointment. ''I came so far . . .''

''I know how frustrated you must feel. I'm sorry.''

''Are there any other lawyers from that era here now?'' Karon persisted. ''Perhaps one of them would know something.''

Steven shook his head. ''My father died five years ago. Only Uncle Mathias remains from that period, and even if he were privy to your case, getting the information out of him might be impossible.'' Steven Peterson explained that his uncle resided in an area rest home. ''Some days Uncle Matt is sharp as a tack when we visit him. He can remember trivial details from the past. Other days he can't remember at dinnertime what he had for lunch. Or if he even had lunch.''

''There's no hope?'' Karon asked dismally.

''There's always hope,'' Steven Peterson assured in a gentle voice. ''I can pay Uncle Matt a visit and ask some questions. Bear in mind, though, I may get no answers.''

Karon smiled weakly. "I'll appreciate whatever you can do. Would you like me to check back? Or would you like my number?"

"Your telephone number would be fine. I'll get in touch if I have any information."

"I'm staying at Derek Eastwood's house. I'm sure it's listed in the book. Or you can reach me through the switchboard at the Timberline Lodge."

Steven Peterson, until that moment, seemed complacent. His eyebrows shot up with shock before he rearranged his expression. Karon was about to make clear it wasn't what it sounded like. Then she decided it should make no difference to Steven what her reasons for being in Derek Eastwood's home were.

The look the young attorney had given her seemed to hint that he hadn't thought her . . . that kind of girl. What kind of woman was she? Karon felt that she no longer knew the answer to that. But perhaps, with the help of Steven Peterson, she would find clues that would enable her to unlock the secrets from the past that barred the door to a happy future.

Karon returned to the Timberline Lodge in time for lunch. When she passed through the lobby she was disappointed to find the office door closed and Derek nowhere in sight. The desk clerk gave her an inquiring glance, but he said nothing about a vacancy and Karon didn't bother to ask.

The fact was that the Timberline Lodge was not preferable to the suite in Derek's home. Karon's rooms there were lovely, with every possible convenience. The downstairs library offered her the perfect work space to face the forms Mrs. Wingate had given her, documents with haunting blanks that cried to be filled with facts she hoped Steven Peterson could present.

The library, Mrs. Sowder assured her when she returned from lunch, was hers to use unless Victoria Dawson needed the room to work on business reports.

Karon spread out her work but her mind wandered for increasingly long periods of time as she stared out the large windows at the white-caps on the lake and her chaotic thoughts drifted.

A feeling of almost physical illness swept over her when she contemplated the thought that Mathias Peterson might not even have the foggiest recollection of the dealings surrounding her unusual adoption. Steven just had to find out something! Anything! If it would only allow her to continue her search for the truth that was so important to her.

Or was it?

Karon's musings reversed. Clawing thoughts took precedence in her mind.

With Chicago and Jon behind her, the burning

urge to discover the truth had cooled. True, she was still curious, but the feeling of frenzy no longer existed. Karon examined her feelings and had to admit to herself that, when she had set out to search her background, in the back of her mind she held tight to the slim hope that her true parents might be nice, respectable people from good families. People she would not be ashamed to claim.

Karon examined her reasons for continuing. Most of them centered on Jon. But it was over between them. Over! So what if Steven found an acceptable family for her to claim? It didn't really matter. She wouldn't return to Jon anyway, because there were so many other differences that drove them apart.

"So there you are!"

Karon hadn't heard the car drive up, nor heard the front door open. Startled she glanced to see Derek Eastwood framed in the doorway of the library, grinning at her.

"You were looking for me?"

Derek's smile was tantalizing and slow. "That's for me to know . . . and you to find out," his lazy drawl had a teasing note. "Actually, I *was* looking for you, Karon." He entered the library. "I seem to have a rather uneventful evening ahead of me. Nothing that can't be put off until tomorrow or handled by Victoria. To spare Mrs. Sowder the trouble—since she would like to see a movie in town—I promised to dine at the lodge. I thought you might like to go with me. We could take a boat ride later.''

"I'd like that,'' Karon accepted the invitation. "I hate eating alone.''

Derek grinned. "You make that sound as if you have two choices—neither very appealing. Either eating alone or suffering through a meal with me just to have a warm body across the table.''

Karon blushed. "That's not what I meant.''

"I should hope not,'' Derek teased. "You'd ruin my self-image!''

"What time will we go to the Timberline?'' Karon asked, sidestepping the awkward moment.

Derek consulted his watch. "Around seven?'' He quirked a dark brow as he waited for her answer.

"Seven is fine. Is there any special way I should dress?''

Karon meant dress for the promised boat ride. She was perplexed by the sudden, strange approval that flooded to Derek's eyes.

"Yes...wear something blue,'' he murmured in a coaxing voice. "And wear your hair up, too, if you would. Just for me...''

Karon was shaken by the intensity of his odd request. "Bu-but a boat ride?''

Derek laughed. "No, for dinner. We'll come

back and change into something suitable for boating.''

''Oh. All right,'' Karon said.

Her voice was shaky, made worse when Derek crossed the room and stood behind her where she sat at the library table. Karon was painfully aware of his closeness and magnetic appeal.

''Wear your hair up, Karon, just for me,'' Derek repeated his persuasive order. ''You've got such a lovely, sleek neck.'' A shiver rippled through Karon when his fingertips grazed her neck and swept her silken hair into a pile of gold curls on top of her crown, baring her graceful neck like an invitation for which Derek Eastwood had no resistance.

Even though in her fantasies Karon expected it, in reality she did not. Karon tensed when Derek's lips dropped to the soft, downy nape of her neck and his warm breath fanned over the tender, sensitive skin. Karon shivered from the contact and was both pleased and disturbed by his touch. For an instant Karon started to give in to the intoxicating touch, then she recoiled, wrenching away from Derek so fast she tipped over the library chair and banged against the table in her haste to get away from him. Her chest heaved as she sucked in a startled breath. Karon's blonde hair, loosely piled up by Derek, spilled around her oval face. She stared at him, her eyes wide, outraged. His were narrowed wih mocking amusement. Instinctively Karon backed away even though Derek did not pursue her.

"Y-you had no right to do that..."

Derek smiled. His eyes glowed. "Perhaps I had no right," he shrugged. "But I did it anyway and I don't regret it. Neither do you, Karon, because you've wanted me to kiss you from the first moment we met. I saw my chance, so I took it. And..."

"And you're...you're..." Karon sputtered. Insulting enough words failed her.

Derek lifted an eyebrow. "Awful?" he suggested. "A rake? A rogue?"

Karon felt like a pouting child being teased and she didn't like it. She glared at him, then lifted her chin and averted her gaze.

"All of that," she said coldly. "And a conniver, too!" Karon faced him boldly. "There *was* a room at the lodge last night. You pulled some kind of trick to get me here!"

Karon's remark took Derek by surprise but he remained unruffled.

"Right you are," he admitted, chuckling. "I've always been a man who knew what he wanted and how best to go about getting it. When I know I want something I let nothing stand in my way. If someone else is in my path and I can't get around them, and they refuse to let me pass. . . then I bulldoze them down going over. Yes, Karon. . . I arranged things."

Karon was chilled by Derek's brutal philosophy, but warmed by the tender desire in his eyes that glowed like gentle flames.

"What. . . I. . . want. . . means little to you?" Karon whispered accusingly.

"What you want and what I want are the same thing," Derek pointed out arrogantly. "Granted, I helped things on a bit. But you wouldn't still be here if you didn't want to be. I didn't force you to accept my invitation. You could have refused."

Karon was fuming, but more angry with herself than with Derek Eastwood when she realized how easily she had played into his hands.

"Last night I was exhausted," Karon pointed out in a defensive tone. "How did I know I could get a room somewhere? In light of that, your offer looked good."

"It was a fair offer," Derek said blandly. "Part of my condition was that you could move back to the Timberline and have the first room available. James said you didn't ask about vacancies." Derek's eyes mocked her. "There's a room available there now. Yours if you want it. You can leave any time you like."

"All right, I will!"

"Go ahead, you little minx," Derek chuckled. "But you'll be back. . . because you want me every bit as much as I desire you."

"That's not true!" Karon whispered, and her flush deepened when the denial came out with less conviction than she liked. For a response, Derek laughed.

Karon shot him an angry look, turned on her heel and marched to her room to dress for dinner, in a yellow gown, with her hair down, just to prove to Derek Eastwood he could not control and manipulate her like a marionette.

Karon hastily packed her bags but did not go so far as to haul her luggage to her car. She would have except that she was afraid James might have already rented the empty room and she couldn't have stood being forced to return to beg Derek's hospitality. There would be time to return for her luggage after speaking with James.

Karon came downstairs dressed in defiance. Derek gave her an amused look, crossed the room and kissed her cheek, taking her hand with a possessiveness even Jon had never used.

"You look lovely, darling."

Derek's words were so sincere Karon felt ashamed she had not worn what Derek Eastwood would have preferred.

Derek helped Karon into his Lincoln, as if there were no question she was going to spend the evening with him. No more was said about Karon's angry outburst, nor of

Derek's crafty manipulations.

During dinner Derek made Karon feel as if she were the only person in the room. In the world. In his life. Derek had eyes only for her and Karon warmed to his admiring gaze and attentive, adoring attitude. Never had Karon enjoyed the present moment so much. And never had the past seemed so far behind, nor the future more remote and unimportant, than when Karon savored each moment in Derek Eastwood's company.

Back at his elegant home they changed into casual clothing. Hand in hand Derek led Karon to the boat dock where his powerful launch was moored. The craft started instantly.

Karon leaned against the cushioned seat. She closed her eyes against the soft mist flung up by the propellers. She enjoyed the caressing breeze that riffled through her hair as lightly as Derek Eastwood's fingers.

It seemed natural, right, when Derek cut the engines and let the large boat drift. From the lake they had a panoramic view of the dark shoreline dotted with glittering lights. Velvety darkness encompassed them.

Derek pulled Karon into his arms. He cradled her head against his broad chest. When Derek's heartbeat quickened to a staccato rhythm, Karon knew it was her effect on the handsome boss of the Timberline Lodge.

Derek slanted Karon's face to his. He paused to study her beauty, then he whispered sweet, husky words and pressed kisses to her closed eyelids, ears, and neck, before he possessively explored the sweetness of her yielding lips.

Emotions unlike any Karon had ever experienced, except with Jon, darted through her. Even though she wanted to retain control of her feelings, Karon felt her resistance slipping away as Derek Eastwood sought to persuade her to accept his wants as her needs.

"Stop...Derek...don't," Karon begged softly. She was surprised, and almost sorry, when he did.

Karon wasn't sure how she managed to get out of his embrace when he took the boat's control again. Karon shivered, uncertain if it were the chilly night air or the after effect of Derek's kisses.

Derek, noticing the chill that passed through Karon on the walk from the beach to his home, put his arm around her. Once inside he went directly to the kitchen.

"What will you have to warm you?"

"Nothing, thanks," Karon said. "But you go ahead."

Derek poured himself a cup of coffee. Karon wandered around in the living room before she took a seat on the sofa, tensing slightly when Derek sat down beside her. He took a long sip

from the steaming mug before he set it aside
and turned to Karon.

"I took the liberty of looking over your papers
while you dressed for dinner," Derek admitted.
"I discovered you're interested in genealogy."

"A little bit, yes," Karon acknowledged.

Derek grimaced. "Some people get great
satisfaction from family trees. I didn't think you
would be one of them—I'm not. I've never considered families all that important. It amazes me
how some people spend pots of money researching so they can brag about the existence of
ancestors long gone from this world."

"Not everyone goes into genealogy for that
reason."

"Perhaps not. For every one of them, there
are probably as many like myself who try to
forget their family's influence. Personally, I get
a royal pain when people rattle off a list of
relatives dating back to the *Mayflower* and act
as if somehow the laurels of the long dead make
family members of the present worthwhile."

"I've known a few people like that," Karon
admitted, but realized Jon hadn't been like that.

Derek and Karon talked about their lifestyles.
Karon was impressed that Derek had attained
a position of wealth and power, not because a
family had arranged it through valuable contacts,
but due to his own abilities and relentless pur-
suit of his goals both in business and private.

"You came here on vacation," Derek said.
"I hope you'll have the sense not to let dead
ancestors keep you from me." Karon's heart
quickened. "There's no sense living in the past,
Karon, and it's foolish to live for the future. The
wisest thing to do is as I do: Live for the moment! It's all any of us really have. Yesterday
is gone—and tomorrow may never come."
Derek drew Karon to him. His eyes seemed to
cast a spell over her. "Live for the moment...and live it with me."

Karon found herself responding to Derek's
kisses. She discovered herself clinging to him,
to his ideas, to his appealing beliefs.

With a gentle strength, Derek's arms tightened around her. Suddenly there was no escap-
ing Derek's lips, his touch, his words.

"I've waited so long for a woman just like
you," Derek whispered. "I had given up hope,
Karon. I knew the moment I saw you that I had
to have you. You knew it, too..."

Derek's touch grew bolder, more demanding.
Karon shivered first from desire, then once
again when she remembered the things Jon had
said that night beneath the stars when he told
her how much he loved her. Jon loved her
enough to take her back to the house...when
nothing was more appealing or tempting than
to remain underneath the stars and protective
darkness locked in each others' arms.

"No...Derek. Don't...don't!" Karon protested, struggling.

"Don't fight me!" Derek pinned her to him.

Karon shrank from him. Her voice went an octave higher with fright.

"Derek, we hardly know each other!"

Derek laughed. "Does it matter how many hours, how many days we've known each other? I knew my feelings for you the instant our eyes met! You did, too. Don't be afraid to become a woman, Karon. I want you, always..."

Karon tried to protest but she was lost, helplessly trapped in an eddying whirlpool of emotion that seemed to pull her down, down, into a strange world that seemed to spin faster and faster as she clung to Derek.

"Always, Karon," Derek breathed when he felt her resistance ebb. "Always and forever..."

# Chapter Eight

"*I* can't believe this phone...!"

Derek's sharp outburst slashed the darkness when the telephone shrilled. With each relentless ring the spell was further broken. Knowing there was no salvaging the intimate mood, Derek abruptly released Karon and crossed the room.

"Hello!" Derek's voice was harsh and his displeasure obvious.

Derek listened, fumbled in his pocket for his cigarettes, produced a lighter, and the soft glow illuminated the room as he played out the telephone cord and carried the instrument to the coffee table. He held the receiver out to Karon.

"For you."

"For me?" Startled, Karon accepted the receiver not knowing who to expect before her hopeful thoughts flew to Steven Peterson. Her expectant greeting was met instead by Midge's brash voice.

"Who is *that*?" Midge asked, dispensing with words of greeting. "And where on earth *are* you?"

Karon glanced at Derek, who pretended not to listen, even as she knew he couldn't help but overhear.

"A friend," she said carefully.

Midge snorted. "Your *friend* sure took his sweet time answering."

"We were only..."

"Spare me the details," Midge suggested. "As long as it took him—I can imagine. Anyway, it's none of my business," Midge said mildly. "It's your vacation. How you spend your time, and with whom, is not my concern. Listen, Karon, I'm calling about Jon. I saw him tonight. He's in a state. He's sick with worry. I think you should..."

"Midge!" Karon cut her off.

"Jon's wild with worry," Midge forged ahead. "The poor guy is wondering if you're terminally ill or in debt to loan sharks and in fear for your life. Karon, he doesn't know what to think—or what *not* to think! How you can doubt Jon's love is a mystery to me. If you could just see how he feels..."

"You seem to forget that how *I* feel counts for something." Karon glanced at Derek.

Midge spoke up. "*He's* right there so you can't talk, huh?"

"Something like that, yes."

Midge sighed. "I don't know what you're up to, Karon, and I'm not sure I would approve if I did. I tried and tried to reach you at the Timberline before they gave me this number. I've been trying all night."

"I was out."

"With Mr. Pleasantness Personified?"

"That's right."

"You're not...seriously involved...are you?"

"No."

"Good," Midge sighed with relief. "And I hope you'll keep it that way. If you could've been a mouse in the corner and seen Jon when he came by, you wouldn't turn your back on a love like this to dally with a whirlwind romance."

"Midge, please!"

"I hope you won't jump into something you may regret. And that you're not planning to forget an old love—and a very good love—with a new flame."

Karon expected Midge to say she was prepared to eat her words regarding that motto, and explain that it didn't apply to everyone. Instead there was silence.

"Midge? Are you still there?"

There was no answer.

In the pale moonlight, Karon saw Derek crouched beside the telephone. His finger depressed the button. He had cut Midge Harper off mid-sentence!

"Midge is going to be hurt!" Karon cried. She'll think I hung up on her!"

"Does it matter what she thinks? What anyone thinks?" Derek asked. "I warned you that I'm an impatient man. I won't let anyone keep you from me. Come to me, Karon..."

Karon's eyes were closed so she didn't see the flash of headlights arc across the dark room when a car swung into the lot. Nor did she hear quiet footsteps on the flagstone path. All she heard were the sweet endearments Derek whispered. Karon was oblivious to the soft rasp of a key inserted in the lock.

She cried in surprise when the chandelier directly above them came on and bathed them in its harsh glare. Karon whirled, expecting to see a flustered Mrs. Sowder. Instead she came face to face with a strikingly beautiful, ebony-haired woman who regarded her and Derek with amused green eyes rimmed with long, curly black lashes.

"Well, isn't this cozy?" Victoria Dawson cooed, and punctuated the remark with a belittling laugh. After the initial look of astonishment had faded, Victoria faced Derek as if she were about to say something, but the warning flash in Derek's eyes made her abandon the idea.

"I've been trying to reach you, Derek, but the telephone must be off the hook on one of the extensions. I kept getting a busy signal. Sara called from St. Paul and said there were problems with the Drescher contract."

Derek cursed softly. "Great, just great," he muttered. "I thought we had that parcel of land wrapped up and secured with a big red bow."

Victoria shrugged. "So did I." She crossed to replace the receiver in the telephone cradle. She sat down across from Derek and Karon. "Apparently Mr. Drescher doesn't feel that way." Victoria examined her manicure and made a face. "You know how he can be..."

"All too well," Derek sighed. "Call Sara back and tell her I'll fly in tomorrow. I'll see Old Man Drescher and try to get things ironed out."

"Very well," Victoria said, rising. "Will you need me to go with you, darling?"

Karon heard the hope in Victoria Dawson's voice. She also saw the hurt that glinted in the woman's emerald green eyes when Derek brushed her offer aside.

"You're needed here, Vic. Stay and get some

sunlight and fresh air. Before long we'll be heading for Las Vegas and you won't have a chance then, when day becomes as night at the casino.''

"All right," Victoria agreed. "I'll be in my quarters, Derek, if you decide . . . you need me.''

Karon stared after the tall beauty when she walked from the room, her back stiff, her hips swaying invitingly. There had been no mistaking the message in Victoria Dawson's eyes—for either of them. One look from Victoria's eyes had told Derek she wanted him, that she was his for the taking, on any terms. Long after Victoria had left the room, Karon was haunted by the glance of intense hatred tossed at her, registering keen dislike of Karon's intrusion in Derek's life.

Derek laughed softly. Karon turned to him, puzzled. He cupped her chin with his fingertips and forced her to meet his eyes.

"Don't let Vic upset you, sweet. She's as jealous as she can be, which is her usual frame of mind. Victoria will no doubt try to discourage you—get rid of you—the way she does any woman who comes into contact with me. Vic is competent and an excellent assistant, so I put up with her insecurities in the same way she tolerates my failings.''

"I see," Karon said in a stiff voice.

"Judging from the look on her face, I'd say

she's intent on getting rid of you. God only knows what she'll say in hopes of doing the trick. But I can't let her get away with it . . . not this time." Derek's voice was hoarse with emotion. "Now that I've finally found you, Karon, promise me that you won't let Vicky's insinuations force you away. Not now that I've found a woman like one I've waited for so long. I couldn't bear to lose you."

"Derek . . ."

He went on grimly. "If Victoria gives you trouble tomorrow, I'll take care of her when I get back. Until then, darling . . ." Derek pressed a quick kiss to Karon's lips, informed her they would dine together on his return, and then he was gone.

Dazed by all that had happened in such a short time, Karon went to her room, but sleep was a long time in coming. Karon was too busy mentally planning ahead for when she was with Derek again. She would wear the flattering blue dress that hugged her figure and swirled around her legs. And she would wear her hair piled high. Just the way Derek would like it.

For a moment Karon was bothered by the way Derek had seemed to order her to have dinner with him. He hadn't asked if she was free. Or if she even wanted to be with him. He expected her to bend her schedule to fit his needs. He commanded her to be with him—

assuming, of course, she would obey.

And . . . he was right.

* * *

Derek was already gone when Karon went downstairs the next day. She was lingering over a second cup of coffee when she heard a noise and turned to see Victoria approaching.

Victoria wore a revealing summer dress of a white and green silk print that emphasized her deep tan and accentuated her eyes. Although her greeting was deceptively warm, the chill never left her gaze. Even when Victoria smiled, hard lines of dislike remained at the corners of her mouth and eyes.

"Good morning, Miss Kirlin. Or may I call you Karon?"

"Please do."

Victoria smiled tightly. "Then you must call me Victoria. Or Vicky." She halted beside the breakfast table. "Do you care if I join you?"

Company, particularly that of Victoria Dawson, was last among the things Karon desired, but good manners prevailed.

"Please do."

Victoria seated herself and fired breakfast instructions to Mrs. Sowder. Karon tried to think of a graceful way to remove herself from Victoria's presence as soon as possible. She studied

Derek's assistant. Victoria was beautiful, with a handsomeness the slim woman obviously worked to retain. Victoria was older than Karon had first thought, within a year or two, either direction, of Derek's thirty-three.

The night before, Victoria had looked younger because of artfully applied makeup and flattering lights. In the harsh glare of day, no matter how she worked to conceal them, brittle lines around her eyes and mouth gave hint to a hard, calculating nature.

Victoria dawdled with her coffee until Mrs. Sowder set a plate before her and then left the kitchen. When the vacuum cleaner roared to life upstairs, Victoria gave Karon a hard look and set down her fork. She folded her fingers together and rested her chin there while she regarded Karon.

"Now that we needn't bother with polite small talk for Cookie's sake," Victoria said in a flat tone, "we may as well get down to business and start being honest with each other. I like you no better than you like me."

Karon gasped at Victoria's bluntness even though it was not untrue.

"I'm not sure I understand what you mean," Karon murmured. "I don't feel I know you well enough to decide if I like or dislike you."

Victoria flicked a wrist to slide her jangling bracelets in place on her slim, tan arm. She gave a harsh mocking laugh.

"Don't hide behind prim and prissy manners. Face it! We're enemies. Stay away from Derek Eastwood, and get out of my territory!"

Karon felt an odd mixture of irritation and pity. "I'm sorry about last night," she began calmly. "I saw how hurt you were to...find us...like you did. Derek assured me later that he's hardly your territory! Perhaps *you* feel that way, but it's not returned. He made clear your involvement with him is mainly business."

Victoria laughed derisively. "I've always been involved with Derek both in business and in private. And I always will be. Derek needs me, Karon, more than he's ever needed any other woman. And...I need him. Sure, sometimes he gets diverted by some cute bit of fluff that catches his fancy. But always, Karon, *always* Derek Eastwood comes back to me."

Karon shrugged. "Derek warned me that you had a knack for driving women away—with lies if necessary."

Victoria dismissed the accusation with a cold smile. Her voice became sugary. "I'm really doing you a favor, Karon, warning you. Derek's a man—with all of a man's desires. He hasn't the strength, nor decency of character, to stay away from you. Derek's always been drawn to pretty, petite, cuddly blonde women. He desperately tries to make them fit his dream, but each one somehow disappoints him, and he casts her aside. Then,'' Victoria's voice became triumphant, ''he comes back to me. I may not be Derek Eastwood's flaxen-haired fantasy woman, Karon...but I'm the one he needs.''

''How lucky for him to have you!'' Karon said flippantly.

''And how nice you see it my way!'' Victoria retorted in kind. ''I won't ask you what you see in Derek. He's got it all: money, looks, power, prestige, and an animal magnetism, plus a zest for living like few possess. You're not the first woman to fall for Derek, Karon. Whatever Derek feels for you—don't delude yourself into believing it's love. He wants you, true, but once he's satisfied those needs, and you disappoint him in some way, he'll move on and leave you behind.''

A chill passed through Karon. ''I-I'll be the judge of what Derek feels for me,'' she stammered. ''And of what I feel for him. I have no intention of staying away from Derek if he prefers I be with him.''

''Oh, that's what he'll want, I can assure you,'' Victoria predicted. ''I'm just warning you that if you're smart you'll stay away from him.''

Karon stood to leave. ''And what if Derek refuses to stay away from me?'' she asked calmly.

''Why...that's easy to predict, my little innocent,'' Victoria said and gave a chiding chuckle. "Derek will break your foolish, trusting heart." Victoria's eyes grew pitying. "Maybe I shouldn't spoil your glorious dreams, poor dear, but really, Karon, you don't stand a chance. You're no match for a man like Derek . . . but I am." Victoria lifted her face and spiritedly tossed her mane of black hair over her thin shoulders as she drew new strength. "I know Derek doesn't love me. I learned to live with that long ago." Her voice grew soft, her green eyes glistened with shiny, unshed tears. "What I feel for Derek will be enough for me. He cares for me as much as he'll ever care for another woman. If you're intent on taking Derek from me, then you'll try no matter what I say." Victoria smiled sadly. "Don't worry about me, Karon. I'm a survivor. I'll live through it as I have before. But what about *you*?" Victoria paused. "Will there be someone to pick up the pieces of your broken heart and help you put your life together? Think about *your* life . . . before you make plans to ruin mine . . ."

Victoria gave Karon a cruel glance, downed the cold dregs in her coffee cup, clutched up her belongings, and fled for the office at Timberline Lodge.

Karon sank back to her chair, stunned. Who should she believe? Derek? Or Victoria? Both were so convincing! But hadn't Derek grimly warned that Victoria would stop at nothing? That she would be ruthless? Hadn't Derek hinted that Victoria was a calculating woman, and a good actress, who could rise to any occasion when the need was presented?

Better than a good actress, Karon decided, as she reached for the coffee cup and dismissed the theatrics that had surrounded the fiery scene. Victoria had desperately sought to protect her territory; she was Academy Award winning material!

"A call for you, Miss Kirlin," the housekeeper said. "You can take it on the kitchen telephone."

"There's been news?" Karon asked, when Steven Peterson came on the line.

"We'll discuss it when you get to my office. Can you find time this morning?"

"When?" Karon asked.

"Any time you can make it; I'll work you in."

"I'll be there as soon as I can," Karon promised.

# Chapter Nine

Karon drove to town wondering if Steven Peterson had found out something from his Uncle Matt, or if he wanted her to come to his office in order to break the news that it was useless.

There were few cars in the firm's parking lot, and only two other people waited in the anteroom. Karon accepted a chair and picked up a magazine. Before she could select an article to read she was shown into Steven's office. Karon tried to guess the outcome from his eyes but his gaze revealed nothing.

"Well?" Karon prompted when she took the seat he offered.

"So far, Karon," he said quietly. "A big nothing."

Karon sighed and stared at a patch of sunlight on the carpet. "I was afraid of that," she whispered.

"I could have told you over the telephone," Steve explained. "But I wanted a chance to chat with you so I would know just what this means to you. Do you want me to pursue other avenues?"

"What happened at the rest home?" Karon questioned back.

Steven gave a sad smile. "Nothing. Absolutely nothing. Uncle Matt's mind was clear last night, a nurse told me when I telephoned ahead, so I rushed right over. But Uncle Matt's concentration nowadays is almost nil. He kept hop-scotching to other topics."

"That's common, I'm sure," Karon murmured. "It's not his fault he can't remember."

"The nurse suggested maybe Uncle Matt would be more alert in the morning. Unfortunately my schedule often keeps me tied up until noon with court cases and appointments. I'm not free to visit Uncle Matt then."

"I would pay you for your time," Karon said, "if you think it is worthwhile."

Steve waved aside her offer. "My wife, Sally, volunteered to go see Uncle Matt. She thought maybe it would strike a chord with him if she could chat with him at length. Sal and Uncle Matt get along famously. Maybe she can reach him where others might not."

"I'm prepared to pay for your wife's time, too," Karon said quietly.

"Sal wouldn't hear of that—and neither would I. Sally visits Uncle Matt regularly; she would be going out there anyway."

"That's sweet of her to change her schedule to help me. Please tell her how much I appreciate it." Steven nodded. "If your wife has no luck . . . then what?" Karon continued.

"That's up to you . . . and how significant this is." Steven Peterson searched her eyes. "Is it terribly important? I know the news was recent. Karon, I hesitate to encourage you with this search if, given time, your emotions will heal. You may discover later that you're just as happy not knowing the details surrounding your birth and . . . placement."

Karon shook her head, too confused to speak, too uncertain to know her answer or give it.

"Does it really matter who your biological mother was? Will you be happier knowing her identity? Will it make the future easier to face if you can find the woman and learn from her why she . . . sold you?"

Karon winced. "I-I don't know."

Karon stared at her hands. Days before she had explained to Steven how terribly important it was. But that was before she had come to feel for Derek Eastwood what she had, or been molded by his philosophies. Sometimes it no longer seemed so important when she realized her relationship with Jonathan Wingate was a dead issue. What the two of them had together wasn't likely to spring to life again if she found decent people populating her family tree. They were parted by too many basic differences. But if she reversed her previous sincerity, Steven Peterson would probably decide she was a vacillating woman who didn't know her mind.

"It seems quite important to me," Karon said carefully.

Steven nodded. "Then you want me to continue?"

"Y-yes . . ."

Steven frowned. "Tell me, Karon, do you have any idea of what your biological mother is like?"

The question hung in the air. A second stretched to become a minute.

"No . . . well, yes, I suppose I do."

"I thought so."

Karon didn't share her ideas—the thought that her mother had been a young girl from a good family, who found herself pregnant. Ashamed and rejected, she went away to live in seclusion, then arranged to sell her baby to the Kirlins so she could start life fresh.

"If we were successful and located your mother—would you want to meet her?"

"I think so. Yes," Karon whispered.

"What if she refuses to see you?" Steven asked bluntly.

"I hadn't considered that possibility."

"Suppose she does agree to meet you. What kind of relationship do you hope to have with her? Have you thought that she might have a husband, other children, and that they don't know of her past? Have you contemplated that your appearance might cruelly disrupt her life?"

Karon miserably shook her head. "I-I assumed she would be glad to see me," Karon whispered. Her voice cracked.

Steven shrugged. "Maybe she would. Maybe she wouldn't."

"I suppose it was foolish of me, but I didn't stop to think that far ahead."

"I thought not," Steven said compassionately. He studied his fingertips and gave Karon a hard look. "Exactly what did motivate you to begin this search on such short notice and with so little thought?"

Karon folded her hands and wished Steven would continue to speak so she could collect her thoughts. Instead, he waited in silence for her to answer.

"I wanted to find my family in hope that I had decent ancestors to claim. For the sake of my boyfriend, and our children, if we married."

"Your boyfriend?" Steven asked, his voice disapproving.

Karon avoided his eyes. "My former boyfriend. He comes from a wealthy, prominent, very influential family. The Chicago newspapers often contain items about his relatives. Recently he asked me to marry him, but I'd die before I'd risk marrying him and then have some heartless reporter dig up sordid facts from my past to use against him. I broke up with him."

"That's your reason? So your boyfriend won't be disgusted or embarrassed?" Steven's face revealed his opinion of anyone who would reject a friend on such a basis.

"Finding out for Jon's sake was only part of the reason," Karon admitted. She plunged ahead trying to salvage the situation. "I wanted to find out for my sake, too."

Steven sighed. "I suppose you suspect that your mother was a pregnant girl from a decent family, rejected and afraid. When a sharp lawyer approached her with a financial deal, she profited from her misery, but lived to regret it."

"You've summed it up well," Karon admitted in a bitter whisper.

"What if you pursue this and discover instead that your mother was a different type of woman—from a black market baby factory? A woman who purposely got pregnant so she could sell you to people willing to pay the price? Regardless of what kind of people they were?"

Karon thought she had arrived at most of the possibilities, but the ugliness of the picture Steven Peterson sketched in shook her to the core. At that instant she realized the truth might be more painful and damaging than the agony of never knowing.

"If the only reason you're tampering with the past is hoping to impress a snobbish boyfriend —and former boyfriend at that—I refuse to go along with it! From what you've told me, Stan and Dorothy Kirlin didn't cause your conception, but they were the man and woman who nurtured you. They gave you love and cherished yours. They cared for you. They raised you to the best of their ability. That, Karon, makes them your *real* parents." Steven paused. "As for that boyfriend of yours—if ancestors are that important to him—he must have sawdust where his brains should be!"

"Jon's not the way you make him sound!" Karon said defensively. "I never told Jon the truth. I couldn't. Jon's mother is all hung up on genealogy. She's doing the Wingate family tree. Plus, the Wingates are all very religious. Christians. If I told Jon the truth he would think he *had* to marry me, even if deep down in his heart, he no longer wanted to. He would feel...obligated.''

''I can understand that the shock makes you doubt everybody,'' Steven conceded. ''But love is love, Karon. We don't always go in search of the people we come to love. Love is an unpredictable emotion that captures us. Different things combine to make love grow. We don't set out to love someone because they're rich, handsome, important...at least we shouldn't...'' Steven grinned. ''Though realistically, I know many people do exactly that.''

Karon nodded. ''Well, you can imagine how Jon's Christian mother would react if he married me and she found out the truth!''

''As a Christian, yes, I can imagine her reaction, as could my wife, Sally. We may have a better understanding of it because we share her viewpoint.'' Steven's voice was gentle. ''A true Christian would never hold something like that against you. Never! If the Wingates are the sincere Christian people you claim them to be, they wouldn't be as bigoted as you fear. I wonder, Karon, if your shock and insecurity didn't make you incorrectly interpret things others said and did.''

''That's possible, I suppose,'' Karon reluctantly admitted.

''I can continue trying with Uncle Matt, if you want,'' Steven offered. ''But I think any answers we might get won't solve your basic problems.

Only by accepting the situation, and understanding your personal worth, will you take care
of that dilemma. When you understand you're
acceptable as an individual, created and loved
by God, He can remove the dark fears that
burden your heart. When you know He accepts
you—mankind's rejection means little. So,
what's your verdict?''

"I-I'd like for you to continue. At least for a
little while,'' Karon said weakly.

Steven looked disappointed but he nodded.
"I'll do what I can. But don't expect
miracles.''

Nodding her thanks Karon quickly left his office. Her eyes were red from tears when she got
into her car and her mind was in a turmoil. She
had no desire to return to the lodge to be seen
in public looking so shattered, and she had no
wish to return to Derek's house and chance Victoria nastily chipping away at her when she
could least withstand it.

Karon drove aimlessly through town in order
to have time to collect her thoughts and control. When she came to the city park, on impulse
she swung her car to the curb. For a few
minutes she watched children play. The rising
sun beat down on the car and warmed the in-
terior. Karon left the vehicle and walked the
sunny paths.

Happy childen squealed as they played. Retired couples out for daily walks gave her bright smiles. Several young mothers pushed children who clung to swings as the tots shrieked, begging their mothers to push them higher, higher!

Karon sat down on a bench. An instant later a young woman approached her.

"Julie!" the woman cried, delighted. "Julie Odegaard, what a surprise! I can't believe it's really you!" The woman caught at Karon's arms and slid to the bench beside her, grinning. "I almost didn't recognize you, Julie. But what's it been? At least five years?"

Startled, Karon faced the woman—a complete stranger. "I'm sorry, but . . ."

"Don't you remember me, Julie?" the woman asked, laughing self-consciously, as her eyes glowed with mild hurt.

Karon shook her head, and tried to frame words. "I'm sorry, but—"

"I was a senior in college when you were a freshman," the woman broke in to supply the link. "We were on the same floor in the dormitory during fall quarter. Now do you remember?"

Karon gave her a pleasant smile. "I'm sorry, but you're mistaken and confusing me with someone else. My name isn't Julie . . ."

The woman studied Karon carefully. "Oh, pardon me," the pregnant woman groaned

Embarrassment shaded her perky features a deep red. "I feel like an idiot gushing at you like I did. I thought you were an old friend. I was so excited at the thought of seeing you again I didn't give you a chance to explain my mistake." She gave Karon a searching look. "I can see now you're not who I thought you were. Please forgive me for bothering you!"

"It's all right," Karon said, returning her smile. "I've done that myself. I think everyone has now or then."

"I suppose so. Well, have a nice day!" the woman said and turned away to summon her children.

A few minutes later Karon slipped behind the steering wheel of her car. She felt strengthened. Her face no longer looked so ravaged. In her heart she sensed Steven Peterson was right. The things he said made sense. Maybe she would be wise to leave well enough alone. The search had only seemed important when Jon was important to her. Now, with Derek in her life, the search seemed inconsequential.

It had been a moment of stubborn weakness that had caused Karon to tell Steven to continue. That and an attempt to salvage her pride in the face of the attorney's Christian logic.

Karon toyed with the idea of pulling over to a corner phone booth to leave word for Steven to bother no more. But she dismissed the idea and drove on. She could tell him the next time he called. She was sure he wouldn't find out anything anyway. And, if by some stroke of genius he did, it wouldn't matter. Not to Derek Eastwood. Nor to her. . . .

\* \* \*

Karon was thankful Mrs. Sowder was busy elsewhere when she returned to Derek's house, and that Victoria was absent.

To pass the time until Derek's return, Karon read, sunbathed, then went to her suite to experiment with her hair and makeup until she knew Derek would approve.

In the late afternoon Karon heard Derek's car in the courtyard below her second-story suite. She looked out and her pulse quickened at the sight of him. After Victoria's insinuations Karon feared that she would see Derek in a different light and discover a dark, sinister side in him. She was relieved it was not so.

When Derek glanced up and caught her eyes, he beckoned her to him. Karon's cold fears melted away beneath the warmth of his kiss.

The seeds of doubt planted by Victoria did not bear fruit. Relieved, Karon kissed Derek with more eagerness than before. Derek noticed the difference. It pleased him as much as the picture Karon presented. He looked her over, head to toe, and found everything to his liking.

"Mmmm...nice!" Derek passed judgment and gave Karon a quick kiss before he released her. "You look as lovely as I knew you would. Now, I want to add the crowning touch," he smiled. "Be a good girl and close your eyes."

"Oh, Derek!" Karon protested.

He was firm. "Close your eyes!"

Obediently Karon's lids slipped shut. Following a soft rasp, Derek's fingertips touched her neck, her ears, the pulse spots at her temples. Karon inhaled deeply.

"Perfume?"

"Perfume. The best," Derek murmured. "For my best girl." Derek noticed the way his words caused Karon to tense. "You jealous little vixen!" he chided in a pleased tone. "You want to be more than my best girl—you want to be my only girl, don't you?"

Karon faced him. Her eyes reflected hurt. Pridefully she lifted her chin. "Is that so wrong?"

"Of course not," Derek whispered. "The way you tensed I knew you were reacting to something more than just words." He sighed. "What's Vicky been up to today?"

Karon gave him a sharp glance. "Nothing,"

she murmured. "Well, nothing you hadn't already warned me about."

"So she did her best to make you so unhappy you'd leave?" Karon nodded. Derek kissed her and held her close. "Maybe Victoria made you unhappy, but I'm here now, and I'll make you happier than you've ever been before, darling. I promise you that!"

"You already have," Karon said simply.

"The perfume?" Derek missed the meaning of her words. "It was nothing."

"Nothing!" Karon cried. "I know the brand. It's so expensive I shouldn't even accept it!"

Derek laughed. "Not only can you accept it, you will. Don't be stuffy and prudish. So what if Emily Post or whoever says nice girls don't accept expensive gifts from gentlemen friends? To you the price may seem costly. To me? A trinket. Anyway, I got it more for me than for you," he explained, "if I can admit to such selfishness. It happens to be my favorite perfume. I want you to wear it for me."

"Well, if you insist," Karon murmured.

Derek gave her a dazzling smile. "I insist," he whispered.

\* \* \*

That week with Derek, time, which would have dragged had Karon been by herself, sped by all too quickly. Karon couldn't believe what time it was each night when Derek brought her home and they parted only a few hours to rest before they awakened to fill each portion of the new day with fun things to do.

"I promised you I'd make you happy, and I do, don't I?" Derek asked.

"Yes, you've made me very happy. So happy that sometimes I feel I'm going to burst with contentment. You've made me feel very special. . . and I love you for that."

At her admission, Karon's heart skipped a beat. She waited for Derek to murmur words of love, instead he tilted her face to his and kissed her until her entire being seemed to ache with sharp yearning.

"I-I really must go," Karon said shakily and broke away from his embrace.

"Yes, you must!" Derek whispered. His eyes were hazy with desire. "Go! Before I force you to stay. . . ."

Each morning Karon was relieved not to confront Victoria Dawson, who seemed to be running Derek's business empire while he kept Karon company.

No matter how early Karon arose, Derek was ready and waiting at the breakfast table. When he set the newspaper aside, he would outline his plans—their plans—and Karon, who hadn't the time to develop ideas of her own about how to spend her day, willingly accepted his desires as her own.

For almost an entire week Karon was with Derek almost constantly: playing golf and tennis, taking boat rides on the lake, or going for short flights over the area so Karon could more fully appreciate the wilderness beauty. Their evenings were spent at the lodge dining before they adjourned to the lounge where they talked, danced, and enjoyed the atmosphere when they were too tired to return to the hardwood floor.

Each night Karon steeled herself for a showdown that did not occur. She expected Derek to start pressuring her not to make their nights together end by going to separate suites. Every evening she found herself suffering mixed reactions, relief and disappointment, when the subject did not arise.

That week Karon saw as much of Derek Eastwood as she saw little of Victoria Dawson. It didn't take Karon by surprise when Derek began to hint that the time was drawing close for him to leave. He hinted that he had hoped Karon would be at his side when he left.

"Do you mean it?" Karon whispered. Her voice went thin with happiness. But the elation she felt was short-lived. When Derek spoke on about her going with him to his Las Vegas casino, she soon realized he wanted her with him...but he said not one word about marriage.

Alone with her thoughts Karon assessed her goals. Marriage had always been one of them. She had planned on the solid, legal, loving commitment. She had also assumed she would wait for the enduring promise marriage offered before giving herself to any man.

That was before Derek entered her life, bringing with him philosophies she never really stopped to consider before. Karon examined her feelings. Nothing seemed orderly or basic any longer. When she pitted the easy ethics Derek offered against her own vague ideals, it was no longer so easy to leave him when he made clear he wished they had no need to part.

Steven Peterson didn't contact Karon that week. Karon hadn't bothered to check for further developments, assuming there were none. Midge Harper had called several times while Karon was out, but Karon ignored Mrs. Sowder's neat notes and postponed returning the calls, deciding it would be easier to face Midge's opinions and lectures at a later date than to face news about Jon or receive unwanted advice.

All week long Karon lived for the moment. On Friday night after Karon and Derek had dinner together, he returned to the house and picked up the weekender bag Mrs. Sowder had packed. Derek prepared to drive himself—and a triumphant Victoria Dawson—to the airport where his private plane was waiting.

"When I come back, Karon, it won't be for long," Derek stressed. "You know that." Karon nodded and glanced at Victoria, who waited in his car. "You also know I want you with me when I leave. You decide what you want from life. If what you want is also what I want . . . we'll face the future together. Think it over. Be ready to give me your answer when I come back."

When Derek left, after kissing her warmly, Karon sensed that, even though the handsome businessman was providing her with time to reach a decision, it had not occurred to him that she might refuse his offer. Already Derek seemed positive that she would go with him. But would she? Even Karon did not yet know . . . .

# Chapter Ten

Karon promised herself that over the weekend she would think about Derek's offer. Instead of weighing her emotions and reaching a decision, Karon was consumed with jealousy that was fueled by vivid, tormenting images of Victoria Dawson alone with Derek—and making the most of the intimate situation. The gnawing thought that she would never be able to trust Victoria, or Derek, no matter what commitment he gave her, further eroded Karon's confidence.

Could she hope to have any kind of solid relationship with Derek? Would she be able to trust him as she should with a heartless, scheming woman waiting in the wings?

Karon didn't know. Yet within days, Derek expected her to have an answer. She knew her choice, right or wrong, would shape her destiny. It was a decision she faced alone.

The weekend without Derek dragged by.

Saturday night Karon returned to the lonely house after a solitary meal at the lodge. When she entered, Mrs. Sowder informed her that Midge had telephoned again. Knowing that she couldn't stall Midge forever, Karon started to dial the number. Quickly she hung up before she completed the sequence, knowing that if Midge bombarded her with questions, she would confess everything she was feeling. Instead of helping Karon to find answers, Midge's opinions might only confuse her more.

When the telephone shrilled as Karon's hand still rested on the receiver, startled, she answered, expecting Midge. Karon was relieved to discover Steven Peterson on the line.

"Sally went to see Uncle Matt yesterday, but she didn't make any headway," he said. "Sal thought maybe if you saw Mathias yourself, and told him about your parents and asked questions, that—"

"It might spark his memory?" Karon finished the thought.

"Sally figures it's worth a try," the attorney said.

"Are you free to go tomorrow?"

"Yes. . ." Karon said hesitantly, abandoning former plans to tell Steven to call off the search. "I'm free all day. I can meet you any time you'd like."

"Terrific! Sally told me to invite you over for Sunday dinner. We can go see Uncle Matt afterward."

"Oh, but I hate to impose," Karon said.

"It's no trouble," Steven said so sincerely that Karon believed him. "We would love your company."

"Well, if you're sure. . . I'd enjoy that very much. How do I find your house?"

Steven gave a set of complicated instructions. Karon's pen raced across the notepad.

"I hope you realize I'll never find you," Karon warned.

"You may be right," Steven replied seriously. "Our home isn't easy for a stranger to locate. I'll tell you what, why don't you meet us at church and follow us home?"

"Good idea. What time do services let out?"

Steven paused. "I. . . thought. . . you might meet us in time to attend with us, Karon, then. . ."

Karon blushed when she realized how she must have sounded.

"Of course," she said quietly. "I'm glad you thought of it. That would be nice."

"We'll see you tomorrow at ten," Steven affirmed, and gave Karon the street address.

"Fine, I'll see you then."

\* \* \*

Sunday morning Karon was up early and dressed with care. She allowed plenty of time and found the street address with no difficulty. Karon swung into the parking lot, smiling at the people who turned to greet her with pleasant faces.

Walking to the front steps, her eyes roved for Steven. She was relieved when she saw him with a cluster of people. When he caught sight of her, he broke away and came to her.

"Karon, it's good to see you!" He guided her to the group and made quick introductions. "Sally and the kids are inside. We're expecting a baby in a few more months. I didn't want her standing in the hot sun."

Steven ushered Karon to a pew where two little boys with sandy hair waited. They gave Karon shy, curious grins. Steven's wife, who read from her Bible as she waited for services to begin, moved down to make room. Sally Peterson glanced at Karon. The smile froze on her face. Karon's lips parted in surprise.

Karon was so startled to find that the woman she had encountered in the park, the one mistaking her for an old friend, was Steven Peterson's wife. She scarcely heard the opening song or the beginning prayer.

Karon had overcome her shock by the time the pastor delivered his sermon. Using the familiar parable of The Prodigal Son, Karon discovered she had never really heard the lesson this story taught. In her younger days, she thought of it as just another story with a happy ending. The clergyman stressed, however, that, just as the father had accepted his wayward son back into the family with open arms, so could anybody be welcomed into God's family. The only requirements were the admission to human frailties and asking Christ to come into our hearts. Since Jesus had already paid the price for all persons, anyone could claim his rightful place in the eternal family by receiving the gift of forgiveness Jesus offers.

For the first time, Karon was inspired by the Scriptures, enough to believe she, too, could have an inherited place in that family. It was an exhilarating feeling.

After services, Steven started to introduce the two women. Sally Peterson laid a restraining hand on his arm.

"Karon and I have already met, although we had no idea at the time. Last week I mistook Karon for a girl I knew in college, so it was a surprise for us to meet again today."

Sally was so warm and friendly that Karon knew she was welcome at their table. Karon was at ease with the pleasant woman and enjoyed the delicious home-cooked meal after the previous week's restaurant fare.

During the meal, Steven and Sally discussed items in the church bulletin and mentioned various projects they were involved with.

"Your pastor is an excellent speaker," Karon said. "Some of the points he made in his sermon seemed almost meant for me."

Steven smiled. "They probably were."

Karon gave him an unsettling glance. "You surely didn't tell him about me...and suggest something did you?" she asked in a small voice.

Steven laughed. "Of course not, Karon. I would never dream of guiding him in his message. But I'm sure the Lord probably did. God knows your problems and cares. He knows what burdens you carry. The Lord knew what you needed to hear, and He inspired the pastor to give that message to us all."

After dinner Karon followed the Petersons to the rest home in her own car. She didn't know what she would face. But with her inner understanding that it didn't really matter what they found out, the visit wasn't as difficult to make.

At the rest home Steven and Sally chatted with their aged uncle, as did Karon. Mathias Peterson was so delighted to have a stranger—and a pretty one, at that—visiting him, that his mind centered on little else. Soon the three gave up trying to get Uncle Matt to unlock the secrets to Karon's past.

"It's the Lord's will," Sally said and gave Karon's shoulder an encouraging pat when they left. "If you're meant to discover the facts surrounding your birth, then in the Lord's own time, you will. Perhaps His purpose is better served by denying what you seek this time so you will look elsewhere for His answer."

Karon nodded. She turned to her car, already bleak at the thought of leaving the warm companionship of the Petersons for the cold, lonely luxury of Derek Eastwood's home.

"Why don't you come with us?" Sally suggested. "We can feast on leftovers. I've really enjoyed visiting with you. I hate to have it end."

"I've enjoyed it, too. Leftovers never sounded more appealing," Karon added, smiling.

When they returned to the neat ranch home, Steven went to his study to make several calls, and Sally sat with Karon in the back yard and watched the boys play in the wading pool.

"Karon, it's really been nice having you spend Sunday with us." Sally smiled warmly as she spoke.

Karon hesitated before replying. "You know, it's been a while since I have been to a church service, mostly because I didn't think any of it applied to me. But I was impressed with the minister's logic today."

Sally looked away from the boys for a moment, meeting Karon's eyes. "That's great, Karon, but how do you *really* feel? What is your relationship with the Lord right *here*?" Sally continued as she placed her hand over her heart.

Karon's eyes dropped to her lap.

"It's really not so important where we have been, Karon, as where we are going with our lives. God wanted us to have life and have it more abundantly. As much as you want to know where you came from, the only lasting peace and joy comes from giving your life to Jesus Christ."

And with that, Sally patted the other woman's arm in understanding, while Karon tried to comprehend all she heard that day.

It was after ten o'clock when Karon left their home and drove to the resort. She yawned contentedly. It had been one of the most pleasant days she had experienced in a long time. After leaving the special snug atmosphere of the Petersons' home, when Karon closed the door of Derek Eastwood's house behind her, she felt unsettled by the world of wealth, power, sophistication, and excitement that suddenly seemed to envelop her.

How confusing it seemed. Her desires swayed back and forth between the two worlds until she didn't know which she really wanted. Or who. When she was with Sally, she felt as if she knew what she wanted: the same things Sally Peterson cherished and enjoyed. Yet, when she was with Derek, his world beckoned with tempting brilliance.

That night Karon tossed and turned a long time thinking over Derek's offer before she decided that maybe she could have the best of both worlds. She might be able to find it all with Derek: love, commitment, marriage, a family, and happiness. Someday. . .

If only she could know for sure there was true hope for those things, she would be able to give Derek the answer he expected. But first she had to satisfy herself that what they had together was love. A love that could withstand anything the future would challenge them to face.

\*    \*    \*

"We can't go on like this, Karon!" Derek said. A hint of exasperation crept into his voice.

Karon sighed and faced him with vulnerable eyes. "I know," she admitted. She knew there was no more stalling for time.

"The time with you has been like heaven on

earth for me, Karon," Derek whispered. He kissed her. "It's been like the answer to a prayer...finding you, having you with me. I want it to never end. But—"

"But you have other business concerns that need your personal attention," Karon finished the statement for him.

Derek nodded. "The Timberline Lodge is just one of my company's holdings. I can't devote all of my time to it..and you..at the expense of my other ventures."

"I'm aware of that," Karon said softly, "and I'm not asking you to."

"It was a quirk of fate that brought me here, to find you, my dream woman, at my lodge. I bowed to fate and stayed longer than I should have. I can't stay here indefinitely. I have a casino in Vegas, a health spa in California, and there's a ski lodge in Colorado I'm in the process of acquiring. I'll have to leave...soon."

"And you want me with you."

Derek heard the indecision in Karon's voice. He then realized her answer wasn't as cut-and-dried as he had believed.

"I want you, yes, and I need you, Karon. I'm a man used to giving orders—not one who has to ask favors. I expected you would go with me." Derek paused. "I didn't stop to think about the life you would be leaving behind. I didn't give thought that you might not want to abandon the past to step into my future.''

"I'm not sure I can," Karon admitted. "Or that I want to."

Derek gripped her shoulders. His eyes bored into hers. "I told you I'd never beg you to be with me. I was wrong! I will beg you, Karon. And I am! Please! I don't think I can find happiness ever again without you."

Karon was startled by the depth of his emotion. "I-I don't know what to say."

"Then say yes!" Derek implored. "I promise you that you won't regret it. We'll travel. We'll meet interesting people. You can afford to visit old friends often. I won't demand all your time. You'll have everything you could possibly want that my money can buy. Give me your love, Karon, and I'll put the world at your feet."

"Derek, I really don't..." Karon's voice trailed off.

He gave her a soft shake. "Don't give me your answer yet," he ordered desperately. "I know sharing my life would be a big step for you. Once you make the decision, there's no turning back. I think you understand that." Karon nodded. "I have to fly to the Twin Cities tomorrow afteroon for a conference. I'll probably take Vicky with me. You'll be alone. You can think then. I'll return the next morning and I'll expect your decision then."

After spending the rest of the evening with Derek, Karon had an unrestful night. It seemed she had only slept a few minutes when sunlight brightened the room to make further sleep impossible.

Karon arose more exhausted than when she retired the night before because of the tangling emotions that tied her in knots, brought battle to all her beliefs, and robbed her of sleep.

Karon considered the things Steven and Sally had said, and heeded the content of the pastor's Sunday sermon. Karon considered many things Jon had said. Midge's blunt opinions came flooding back, too. Karon dwelled on what Derek Eastwood offered. She tried to think of what life would be like without him. Then she tried to imagine what their day-to-day relationship would be like if they lived for the present, moment by moment building a future together.

By the time Derek was ready to leave for the airport that afternoon, the scale was tipping in his favor. Karon's bright vision for the future was marred only by the dark shadow of doubt she suffered after detecting the remnant of a smug smile on Victoria Dawson's face. Vicky would be accompanying Derek to the airport.

Karon, who had never before known jealousy, suffered agonizing pangs of envy and her
imagination ran wild. When Derek and Victoria
left together Karon stared after the car and
wondered idly if Derek's desire to have her with
him was strong enough to make him send Victoria Dawson away!

Unable to stand the confines of Derek's home,
Karon took to the beach, walking what seemed
like miles. The time was spent in heavy thought,
but Karon still found no answers. Logically she
knew she should tell Derek yes—and accept all
he had to offer. But one small part of her romantic heart refused to agree. . . .

Karon was startled when she returned to the
house to find Victoria Dawson curled up in
Derek's favorite chair reading. Classical music
emanated from stereo speakers strategically
located throughout the house. Victoria looked
up and smiled.

Derek's beautiful assistant had seemed
gloating when she left with him. Suddenly upon
her return, Vicky was so subdued it startled
Karon to discover the change so she scarcely
knew what to think.

Victoria started a conversation and Karon took
part. At any time Karon expected disdain to
creep into the black-haired beauty's manner,
but Vicky remained friendly. Eventually Karon
concluded that Derek had given his willful,

headstrong assistant a stiff message. No doubt he had laid it on the line to Victoria that Karon was in his life for good if she chose to be, and that if Vicky knew what was good for her, and valued her job, then she had better gracefully accept the situation.

Whatever the reason, something had changed Victoria's attitude and Karon appreciated it. She still felt a sense of hesitancy, though, when Victoria suggested they take a late dinner together at the lodge since neither had eaten.

It was after nine when they were served. They savored the cuisine, then lingered over coffee as they chatted about clothes, movies, and good books they had both read.

One by one Karon's reservations began to fall away. If Victoria Dawson could be counted on not to meddle and start trouble, there would be nothing to cripple Karon's chances of finding happiness with Derek.

When the two women returned to Derek's home, Victoria, like Karon, seemed reluctant to have the pleasant night end. After summoning Mrs. Sowder to bring coffee, Victoria kicked off her elegant sandals and curled up on the sofa.

"I was in the library the other day and saw your papers," Victoria began. "Forgive me for being nosy, but I couldn't resist a look. I didn't know you were into genealogy. Having any luck?"

"Not much," Karon said, and decided against explaining that she was content to stop her search before she really got started.

"It's a lot of work," Vicky made a face. "Several years ago my grandmother got involved in all that when it was the latest craze. Gran spent a lot of time and quite a bit of money. She had a grand time doing it, though, or obviously she wouldn't have taken the trouble. Gran saw it through to completion where I'm sure many don't, and she had a family history book printed. I have a copy. It's interesting, if you enjoy that kind of thing."

"I'm sure it's nice to pass on to younger generations."

"It is," Vicky agreed. "Are you having any success in finding relatives in this area?"

"I . . . haven't found any yet. But I haven't really taken the time to find out."

Victoria gave Karon a studied appraisal. "With your blonde hair and blue eyes—very probably you have relatives here—what with all the Swedes and Norwegians in the area. Sometimes it seems when you go to small towns everyone is related to everyone else." Victoria stretched with a lithe grace of a sleek jungle cat and yawned.

"I suppose that's true," Karon said.

"You really haven't had time for your genealogy. Derek's kept you so busy!" Victoria said.

Her eyes narrowed with suspicion. "Hmmm . . .
maybe he's kept you busy for a reason!" Victoria gave Karon a glittery, amused smile.
"Perhaps Derek is afraid if you poke around
in the area you'll discover that you're related
to his wife." Victoria gave a chilly laugh.
"Derek's wife was from these parts. That's
how Derek came to have a resort in the Minnesota wilds."

Karon's heart stopped beating. The blood
rushed to her temples. Her pulse hammered and
her chest felt too tight to allow her to draw a
breath.

*"Wife?!"*

"Oh, it wouldn't surprise me at all to find out
you're related to her," Victoria went on airily
as she intently studied her nails. "You and
Derek's wife favor each other a great deal in
looks."

"Wife . . ."

Karon's whisper was sodden, numb. Tears
sprang to her eyes. She blinked them back,
clenching her hands until her nails dug into her
palms to keep from crying. She wouldn't give
Victoria Dawson the perverse satisfaction of
bringing her to tears!

Karon very much wanted to believe the awful
news was a cunning lie, but in her heart she
knew it was true. No wonder Mrs. Sowder had
been disapproving on sight! That explained

why Derek never spoke of marriage. He was already married! Somewhere, another woman—his wife—waited.

Victoria grinned at Karon's stricken reaction. Victoria casually raked her fingers through her glossy hair and flung it over her tanned shoulder, bracelets jangling. She took a last puff on her cigarette and brusquely ground it out in the ashtray, breathing words along with smoke.

"Uh-oh," she said. "It looks like I spilled the beans. Derek is going to be furious." She yawned, revealing her unconcern with his anger. She shrugged her slim shoulders. "I suppose he planned to tell you about his marriage in his own way and time, but I figured you already knew."

Karon found her voice. "No. . . no, I didn't. But I'm very glad you told me."

Victoria frowned, puzzled. "Are you? It makes a difference to you?" Karon sensed that to Victoria it did not.

"Yes. . . it most certainly does."

Seconds dragged by like days. Karon couldn't remember what she or Victoria talked about, or if they even spoke.

Karon had no conscious recollection of her actions until she went to her room to pack. Instead, heartbroken, she fell sobbing to the bed.

**Even as Karon tried not to believe Derek was**

married, her heart understood that he was. The facts added up. Derek was a man to whom family ties meant little. Obviously his marriage vows meant no more.

Karon felt sluggish and emptied of life when she raised herself from the tear-dampened bed to find it was well after midnight. How incredible to realize that only hours before she thought she knew her heart and decision! Victoria's news made her world turn upside down.

Like it or not, Karon still felt attracted to Derek. Those feelings hadn't died the moment she learned the truth. Maybe his marriage made no difference to Victoria. But Karon could never cast everything aside to roam the country, jetting from one luxury spot to another, content only to be with Derek and live for the moment when she knew that somewhere another woman waited with a heart that was probably as heavy as her own.

Karon shuddered from her thoughts. How close she had come to playing into Derek Eastwood's hands. Leaden realization dragged her down, even as thanksgiving lifted her spirit to know that she had not prematurely given Derek Eastwood the gift of herself. A gift he was not free to accept and cherish. A gift it was not yet right for Karon to bestow.

Derek Eastwood couldn't give her the things

Sally Peterson treasured—family, home, a loving husband, and most of all, a living faith—things Karon realized she wanted very much. But somewhere, someday, Karon trusted, she would meet a man, the right man, one who could.

# *Chapter Eleven*

*H*er mind made up, Karon wrestled with her luggage. She made her way down the curving staircase to the front door. Noiselessly Karon stepped out and closed the door behind her.

Brakes squeaked. Red lights flashed. A taxi-cab halted in front of the magnificent home. A dark shadowy figure stepped into the night. Words and money exchanged. The yellow cab sped away, and the man came up the walk.

Derek was home. *Early!*

Karon's heart hammered wildly. Abruptly she made her way down the flagstone walk and breezed past him. Derek turned, shocked, and clutched at her arm when he recognized her.

Frantically Karon shook herself free from his touch.

"Karon, what on earth are you doing?"

Karon glanced at him, choked on explanatory words and sobs, miserably shook her head, and plunged toward her car.

Derek's hands fell away from her to hang at his sides. He stared at her a horrified moment before he sprang into action and hurried after her. He caught up with Karon and moved to block her path. She darted determinedly around him.

"Karon, what's wrong? Please tell me! I think I have a right to know."

Karon's voice shook with anger and hurt. Her eyes glowed. "There are things I think I had a right to know, too!" she said in a fierce, furious tone. Her voice softened and became tremulous before it cracked on a sob. "Why didn't you tell me you were married, Derek? *Why?*"

A rainbow of emotions colored Derek's face, revealed by the pale glow from the patio lights. His complexion drained and grew waxen. Derek looked stunned. When his color returned, it brought with it fury. He swore softly.

"Okay." His voice was harsh. "What did Victoria tell you about my wife?"

Karon refused to look at him. She flung her belongings about in order to cram them into the skimpy trunk.

"Oh, nothing really," Karon said in a brittle voice and shot him a cold glance. "She just mentioned you were married. She told me by accident—because she assumed I already knew!"

Derek sighed. "It was no accident. But we won't quibble about that. All right, you know about my marriage. Now do you want to know about my wife?"

"Yes!" Karon snapped before she could think. "No!" she changed her mind as quickly. "Skip it. It doesn't make any difference."

"I'll tell you anyway," Derek said flatly. He gripped Karon's arm and pulled her into the house as she struggled against him. His lips were tight with smoldering rage.

"Sit down!" he ordered sharply.

"No!" Karon refused stubbornly. But she sat down anyway before her knees could buckle from under her. Derek sank into a nearby chair. Savagely he jerked the knot from his tie.

"All right," he began in a soft, pained voice. "I'm going to tell you about my wife."

Karon steeled herself to hear the tired, worn out cliches, the familiar excuses given for adultery. She braced herself for a whinning, self-serving story about a cold, uncaring wife, a dead marriage, and the sad admission that theirs was a marriage in name only, for social convenience.

Karon was not prepared for the agony that edged into Derek's voice. A film of wetness made his eyes gleam.

"My wife was from these parts. I met her when she came to work for my firm as a secretary after she spent a year in college. I married her a few months later. I loved her very, very much. When she was killed—flying to California to meet me when the jetliner crashed—a part of me died, too, Karon."

"Derek, I'm sorry . . ."

"Victoria told you I was married," he continued in a heavy voice. "It seems it slipped her mind to explain that I'm a widower. Losing my wife was like losing myself. I've loved no woman since. I thought no woman could ever compare to my wife, or become what she was to me. Then, Karon, you came into my life."

Karon was overcome with sympathy. Even though Derek no longer had tears in his eyes, Karon did. The agony she saw in his rugged features was like pain of her own. With his explanation, Karon saw everything in a different light, not through the glow of half-truths Victoria had presented in such a distorted manner.

"I'm sorry, Derek. So very sorry."

Derek took a deep breath. "Victoria is the one who is going to be sorry," he promised. "If

I hadn't come back early her trick would have worked! You're not the type to play around with married men—I know that. It must have been terrible for you when Vic told you what she did.''

Dark clouds lifted from Karon's horizon when Derek drew her close and kissed her cheek.

''It was. I'm so relieved to know things aren't like she said. I was terrified they were.''

''Why...terrified?'' Derek asked softly, urgently.

''Because...''

''Because you love me?''

''Yes, because I love you,'' Karon said. ''At least I think I do.''

A smile lifted the corner of Derek's mouth. ''You mean you don't know?'' he scolded teasingly.

Karon met his yes with seriousness. ''Right now my world is still spinning. I hardly know what I think or feel. All I know is that I'm very happy there aren't other women, in other places, awaiting your return.''

''Never, darling, never,'' Derek promised tenderly. ''Now that I've found you, you're the only woman I'll ever want. The only one I'll ever need to fill the emptiness in my heart and make me happy again. Marry me, Karon, I want you so very much...''

Days earlier those words would have made Karon's decision an easy one. Now they seemed to arrive too fast on the heels of her hurt and disillusionment. As much as Karon wanted to give Derek an answer right away, for his sake—for her sake—it had to be the right one.

Marriage was forever...

"I don't know what to say."

"Then say nothing tonight!" Derek ordered tenderly. "I've waited for a woman like you for so long I can wait longer. I want you with me as my lover, but now I know I want you as my wife as well. Sleep on it tonight, darling. We'll face it together in the morning..."

Derek was so understanding Karon felt a swift rush of tenderness. Impetuously she drew him closer and her lips gratefully sought his. Derek sighed softly and clung to her, burying his face in the warm, perfumed hollow of her throat. Shakily he forced himself way and held her at arm's length.

"Go!" he commanded in a soft, agonized whisper. He smiled crookedly. "Go now, before I force you to stay!"

Like so many other nights, sleep eluded Karon after she slipped between the satin sheets. Romantically she imagined her life ahead, married to a passionate, interesting, volatile, loving man like Derek Eastwood, who desired her not only as his lover, but yearned to make her his wife.

His wife...

*Mrs. Derek Eastwood!*

They would be happy, she vowed. She and Derek would have a permanent home somewhere, because children needed a stable environment. She would see to it that Victoria Dawson would only be involved in the outer fringes of their life. With the promise of marriage, Karon knew Derek would give her everything she wanted in life. The things Sally Peterson cherished, and much, much more.

Once Karon reached her decision she could hardly wait for morning to come, and with it, the chance to give Derek her answer.

Knowing Derek to be an early riser, Karon rose at dawn and dressed in the only clothing in her room—the outfit she had on as she prepared to leave the night before. Her luggage was still in the trunk.

By seven-thirty Mrs. Sowder was up banging around in the kitchen. The odor of fresh coffee wafted through the house. Karon could make out an occasional mumbled word when Derek spoke as he scanned the morning newspaper.

Karon checked her reflection one last time. Her heart soared with joy when she went down the staircase and made her way to the sunny breakfast nook to give Derek her decision.

Noiselessly Karon padded across the living room carpet. She drew near the nook. Thank goodness Mrs. Sowder was nowhere in sight! Derek was alone and the private moment she counted on was hers.

Just when Karon was about to enter the room, she was halted by Victoria Dawson's voice. She stopped, shaken, hoping that whatever business it was Victoria had with Derek would be dispatched quickly, and she would leave, allowing Karon the intimate moments she desired.

There was heavy silence in the breakfast nook. Karon stood mute, out of sight, not knowing if she should clear her throat to make her presence known, or retreat and come back later. She did neither. When Victoria spoke again, her voice was low and trembling with anger. Karon was helpless to leave.

"You're a fool, Derek Eastwood. A fool!" Victoria snapped. "I'm not going to let you throw away your life and ruin mine in the process."

Derek laughed. "There's little you can do about it, my sweet. I've asked Karon to marry me—and she'll accept. I want her. I always get what I want. I will this time, too."

"No, you won't," Victoria warned grimly.

"Because I refuse to let you get away with it!"

Derek chuckled softly. "I hate to pull rank on you, Vic, but I really don't think you can stop me. Get in my way, sweetheart, and I'm warning you that you've got a lot to lose. I can guarantee that."

Victoria's retort was a scornful laugh. "Maybe you think you'll have Karon, poor darling, but you won't. You can't! After I finish telling Little Miss Innocent the facts—the whole sordid truth—she won't have you on a silver platter!"

"The truth?" Derek questioned. "What petty pack of lies do you have up your pretty sleeve this time?"

Victoria sniffed. "Innocence does not become you, darling. You know perfectly well what I'm talking about." Victoria's voice was a lethal purr.

Silence stretched between them.

"You. . .wouldn't. . .dare!" Derek's voice was almost inaudible. "Vicky, you *wouldn't*!"

Victoria's voice was taunting. "Oh, wouldn't I? Try me and find out! I'll do anything to protect my interests. I've given a lot of my years to furthering your life and business. Before—and after—Julie. It's me you need, Derek, but you're too wrapped up in your sentimental hearts-and-flowers memories to face it. You were facing it, Derek, until you met Karon. All she is to you is a reflection of love. Karon is your dream. . . but I'm your reality. The only reason you want Karon is because she's a mirror image of Julie!"

"Victoria!"

"Oh, admit it, Derek!" Victoria demanded thunderously. "Go ahead and admit to me what you've surely allowed to yourself. You don't love Karon. You adore the way she looks. Or, to be brutally frank—the way you've made her look with your careful suggestions for clothing and hairstyle, right on down to coaxing her to wear Julie's brand of perfume. The natural resemblance to Julie was uncanny. But after Karon took your wishes to heart—it was like seeing Julie Eastwood raised from the dead!"

When Victoria ran out of words, Derek spoke in a flat, begrudging tone. His gold lighter clicked sharply as he flipped it open.

"All right," he exhaled the words. "I'll admit it. You're correct. So what?" His voice was cold. "I don't love Karon. But I never once said I did. I do *want* her. . . and I've told her that."

Victoria's laughter was as shrill as shattering glass.

"Being wanted isn't enough for a girl like Karon. Maybe it's enough for a heartless pragmatic like you—but not for a romantic like her. I was all prepared to dislike the girl on sight, but Derek, she's a nice person and she really doesn't deserve to settle for less than the best. That's all you could ever give her, no matter how many material possessions you showered on her. You don't love Karon. And love is what she needs before all else." Victoria sighed. "You don't love me, either. But I learned to live with that fact long, long ago."

"I don't love Karon now . . . but I believe I can make her into a woman I can love. She's got such potential."

"Potential!" Victoria spat the word. "Of course she's got potential, you blind idiot! Or did you know that she shares the same birthdate as Julie? They're the same height, the same build, coloring. In looks they're as alike as two peas in a pod. Karon, like Julie has roots in this area. Julie was adopted at birth. So was Karon. Add it all up, Derek, and it's not hard to figure out Karon and Julie are identical twins, parted at birth for some reason, adopted into different homes. Small wonder you saw potential in her!"

Derek gasped.

Karon reeled and clutched at the ivy-twined room divider for support to keep from collapsing as the stunning news hit her with full impact.

"How do you know that?" Derek murmured.

Victoria's voice was smug. "Oh, I suspected it almost right away. When I found Karon's papers in the library, I peeked and compared it with what I knew about Julie. I've always been good at math. In case you've forgotten, Derek, two plus two equals four..."

"I can't believe it." Derek was dazed.

*"Do!"* Victoria urged sweetly. "No wonder you want Karon. She's the closest you've ever come to finding Julie's perfect replacement. If you married Karon and she found out she was only a reflection of your previous love for Julie, it would kill her."

"What are you—?"

Victoria rudely cut him off. "Either you tell her that the marriage is off, Derek, and give her whatever reason you like, or I'll tell her the truth! The choice is up to you. And don't think I won't use this trump card. I'm getting older, and my opportunities to work my way up the ladder with another firm are limited. I've invested a lot in you. I intend to stick around to collect the dividends. You need me, Derek, and I need you. I've learned things from you, darling, and one thing I have learned well: I will let nothing, and nobody, stand in the way of what I want!"

"Victoria!" Derek protested in a pleading voice.

Her voice grated harshly. "I mean it! Tell her!"

Karon entered the room. Her pale face was pinched with strain. Unable to speak for a moment, she stared from one to the other. Derek's mouth dropped open in horror.

"No one has to tell me anything," she said in a calm whisper. "I believe I've heard quite enough!"

Karon turned and left Derek Eastwood's home with dignity.

A small, stubborn, human part of her wanted Derek to come after her, tell her it wasn't true, and beg her to stay. But in the fullness of her heart, Karon was relieved, rejoicing, when he did not.

Karon drove away from the massive home where she had known such happiness and experienced such pain. She drove to a scenic area overlooking the placid lake where she parked her car, surprised that her eyes remained dry.

She wondered if tears would come.

Karon thought, she remembered, and she prayed.

A new realization suddenly swept over her. She had been seeking a heritage, for roots somewhere in her past. But she knew now that she had really been searching for something deeper, more basic—a personal relationship with her Creator. A verse she had heard that Sunday morning in church came to her now: "For God so loved the world that He gave His only begotten Son that whosoever believeth in Him should not perish but have everlasting life."

When Karon opened her eyes she felt strength, a new strength, seep over her. She knew then that she would shed no tears over Derek Eastwood, not when new understanding, joy, and the peace of Jesus Christ so totally filled her being. She had suffered pain, but as Jon had so often said, it was not without purpose.

Karon reflectively stared out over the water for a long, long time. She watched the whitecaps disrupt the deep blue serenity with eternal regularity, as sorrow interrupts happiness in life. Karon grasped the magnificent care and detail with which the Creator controlled His universe. With loving presence, the Lord was accepting rule of her life. Christ had patiently waited to guide her, knowing well the weaknesses and vanities of her life that resulted in human failings as she valiantly tried to guide her own course and life for the moment. With His wisdom, Karon saw a glorious future, brilliant beyond the scope of her sweetest dreams.

Understanding came, and with it, bittersweet tears of perfect realization. Things Jon had so patiently tried to convey took on deep meaning. She had heard him then with her ears; now she understood in her heart.

Things Steven Peterson had said took on new life. Karon knew that she belonged. She was accepted. She had a family—the family of God.

Karon's eyes were brimming with happiness. Her heart was full, so full of such rich love. Suddenly she understood so many things. Karon ached to be able to express it all to Jon. At the moment she knew she had never loved him more.

Karon dried her eyes and switched on the ignition. Strengthened, she drove back to the Timberline Lodge. Karon spoke with James, the desk clerk, in the deserted lobby. He was surprised when she insisted on paying for her stay. Karon vowed that Derek Eastwood, who had offered her so many worldly things would give her nothing.

The clerk gave Karon a sad, knowing smile when he took her money.

"By the way, miss, a fellow called here a short while ago and asked for you."

Karon frowned. "Did he leave his number?"

"No. He said he would call back later."

"It was probably a friend in town," Karon said, thinking of Steven Peterson. "I'll give him a call before I leave."

"Use the desk phone if you like."

Karon checked her watch, realized Steven wouldn't be at his office yet, so she consulted the directory and dialed his home. Sally answered. When Karon asked if Steven had tried to get in touch with her, she learned it was not he who had telephoned.

"What's wrong?" Sally asked, sensing something momentous in Karon's life. "Something's happened—hasn't it?"

"Yes."

"Do you want to talk to someone?" Sally asked. "Can I tempt you to meet me for coffee? I have a doctor's appointment later this morning. The sitter is due any minute."

"I'd like that," Karon agreed.

"Wonderful! Where should we meet?"

"Anywhere," Karon said, glancing at James, "as long as it's not at the Timberline Lodge."

"There's the Wilderness Inn, the Birch View, the Log Cabin Lodge," Sally suggested.

"The Birch View is fine," Karon decided. "I'll meet you there."

* * *

The coffee shop of the Birch View was emptied of early morning breakfasters by the time Karon slipped into a booth to wait for Sally. She didn't have long to linger before her friend arrived and took a place opposite Karon.

"I'm so glad you agreed to see me." Sally's frown eased to a smile. "Steve and I have both been worried about you. We've been remembering you in our daily prayers."

Karon smiled weakly. "Sally, have you figured it out?"

"I-I think so," Sally began. "A few days ago I called an old college chum to find out what happened to Julie Odegaard. Pieces started to fit in place. I learned Julie married Derek Eastwood. Later she died in an airplane crash. As much as you look like Julie, when I learned that, I suspected Derek was using you to replace her."

Karon nodded. "He was," she admitted, surprised to learn it didn't hurt as much as she thought to confess it. "Did you...figure out...Julie was my...twin sister?"

Sally nodded. "I knew you were adopted, and Julie was, too. When you spent Sunday with us, you mentioned your birthday and I discovered it was the same date as Julie's! I probably wouldn't have remembered her birthday after all these years, as I've forgotten birthdays of the other girls on the dorm floor, but Julie's was the day before my youngest brother's birthday. It made it easy to remember. I told Steve that night I was positive you were Julie's twin, and that your mother decided to...double her money.

Even if it meant parting twins."

"That's probably as valid a reason as any."
Karon lifted her gaze. "I was a reflection of
Derek's lost love. I know he tried to use me.
But I'm not guiltless on that charge. I was in-
fatuated with him." Karon sighed. "But I didn't
love Derek, either. I was using him to try to
forget the man I truly love. The man I hope still
loves me . . ."

Karon felt a strong, gentle hand on her
shoulder.

"I do still love you, Karon, and I will, always,
and forever. No matter what."

*"Jonathan!"*

Karon whirled, blinking in surprise, hardly
daring to believe it was Jon and not an appari-
tion. He grinned at her and his hazel eyes
brimmed with love, forgiveness, and understanding.

"How?" Karon gasped, remembering her
sharp order to Midge. "How on earth did you
find me?"

Jon gave her a warning grin. "Don't you dare
get mad at Midge! She kept her promise, Karon.
She didn't *tell* me where you were." His eyes
twinkled. "But she did make a point of leaving
a Timberline Lodge brochure on the coffee table
when I came to see her."

"That Midge!"

"She was only doing what she thought was

right," Jon said. "I hope you won't be angry with her."

"How could I be?" Karon cried, laughing. "When I'm so grateful! That explains that—but how did you find me *here*?"

Jon grinned. "A piece of cake, darling. The clerk at the Timberline told me he heard you agree to meet someone at the Birch View. He said if I hurried I could probably catch you here. I walked in just in time to hear you say you still love me. Enough, I hope, to trust me with your problems."

"I do trust you, Jon. More than I can ever tell you."

Karon hardly remembered Sally's departure, nor was she particularly aware of the circumstances as she left with Jon. He parked at a rest area on a bluff overlooking the lake.

"Do you feel like talking about it?" Jon prompted.

A torrent of words flooded forth.

"I was a miserable ball of nerves when we went to see your parents," Karon continued on. "And I'm sure I was unbearably touchy."

"A little," Jon admitted with a smile.

"I misunderstood everything everyone said. I was suspicious of every action. I decided your mother hated me on sight, and purposely humiliated me at dinner. Also, when Liz insisted she discuss something with you, I was sure it was a last-ditch attempt to talk sense into you and point out how wrong I was and how I would never fit into the Wingate family."

Jon groaned. "Oh, Karon . . . not at all!" Jon's eyes showed his dismay. "Liz simply wanted us to plan our parents' surprise anniversary party this fall. It wasn't at *all* what you thought!"

"When your mother told me it was you who got her started in genealogy, part of me died. I knew it must mean something to you."

Jon shook his head and chuckled. "It sure did! It meant the difference between an A or a B in my history class."

"Jon . . . really?" Karon asked in astonishment. He nodded. "I never thought it could be something like that. As interested as your mother was in my roots, I was afraid of everyone learning I was a black market baby. I just knew your mother could never accept *that*."

Jon sighed. "Not only could Mother accept it," Jon said. "She, of all people, would understand. Mother knows the sadness you bear, Karon. Did you stop to wonder why she researches the Wingate line, but not her own? It's because she was raised in a Chicago foundling home, abandoned as a baby. She doesn't even have an adoptive family to claim for her own."

Karon's eyes sparkled with tears when she

realized that Althea Wingate wasn't an enemy but would probably be her most supportive friend.

"Karon, do you remember the day I asked you to marry me?" he asked quietly. She nodded. "I knew then that whatever it was that was bothering you that you and I could never be truly one until we shared a deep commitment to Jesus."

"When I ran away from my problems," Karon whispered, "I was only half a person. I tried to make my life complete. But only after I was emptied, drained, broken, did I see that it was only through faith in Jesus Christ that I could be made whole."

"It was the answer to the prayers of many, many people, Karon. My family has prayed for you often."

"And all of your prayers have been answered. I see now that the Lord protected me even when I didn't know I wanted or needed His care. God guided me and kept me safe. He kept me free that I might someday fully give myself to a Christian man."

He pulled her close and her happy thoughts swirled as he kissed her. Mentally she made a note that she would record that precious moment, the date, and the year, in her Bible—for her children to cherish. And she promised that she would make note of all the milestones she and Jon passed as they traveled the road of life together, led on, guided, comforted by their Lord.

"Jon, you showed me the way through your love. You showed me God's love." Then in the silence, with all the tenderness she felt inside, she touched his face and looking into his wonderful eyes whispered, "I love you, Jon."